GOAT GAME

GOAT GAME

THIRTEEN TALES FROM THE AFGHAN FRONTIER

WICKLIFFE W. WALKER

ISBN-13: 978-1479320479
ISBN-10: 1479320471
Library of Congress Control Number: 2012917399
CreateSpace Independent Publishing Platform
North Charleston, South Carolina

This is a work of fiction. Names, characters, places, and incidents either are the product of the author's imagination or are used fictitiously, and any resemblance to actual persons, living or dead, businesses, companies, or events is entirely coincidental.

Interior imagery enhanced by Andi Kulbacki of ABSOLUTE IMAGES! in Washington PA.

ALSO BY THE AUTHOR

Courting the Diamond Sow: A Whitewater Expedition on Tibet's Forbidden River (nonfiction)

Paddling the Frontier: Guide to Pakistan's Whitewater (nonfiction)

From this volume the following stories previously appeared in the quarterly *The Country and Abroad*: "Goat Game," "The Freedom of the Press," "Ringing in the New," "A Schoolhouse for Nuristan," "My Feral Uncle," and "This Troublesome Priest." The author is deeply grateful to publishers Elizabeth Backman Potter and Donn King Potter for their support.

ACKNOWLEDGMENTS

You know who you are.

...if he knew when it was their honour to stand by him, and when it was their honour to betray him; when they were bound to protect and when to kill him—he might, by judging his times and opportunities, pass safely from one end of the mountains to the other.

—Winston S. Churchill,
The Story of the Malakand Field Force, 1898

CONTENTS

FOREWORD

Most Americans are well aware of our deep, costly involvement in Afghanistan these past eleven years since the 9/11 terrorist attacks on our nation. Few Americans, however, realize that our commitment to that poor, war-wracked nation formally began on Christmas Eve 1979 when the Soviet Army invaded Afghanistan. Their aim was to achieve a centuries-old goal to bring Afghanistan firmly under Moscow's control. That act of blatant aggression sparked the formation of the Mujahedin, an internal Afghan resistance movement to the Soviet invaders. In small groups these patriots took to the mountains, fighting a twelve-year jihad against the Soviets and their Afghan communist puppet government.

Within weeks of the Soviet invasion, the United States, in partnership with the government of Pakistan, organized a clandestine program to provide assistance—weapons, ammunition, food, medicine, and training—to the Mujahedin. With the Mujahedin victory in Kabul in April 1992, and the following formation of a democratically elected, Mujahedin-based government, formal US involvement in Afghanistan ended. Over the next nine years, the CIA maintained low-level contact with a few former Mujahedin commanders and sent small teams of CIA officers into northern Afghanistan in mid-1997. These maneuvers kept the door open for the US Government to renew full involvement with the anti-Taliban Mujahedin commanders in late September 2001.

While numerous books have been published dealing with US involvement on the ground in Afghanistan following 9/11, these works focus primarily on overt military efforts by the CIA and US Special Forces to defeat the Taliban. Virtually nothing is available that tells the story of how the decades-long shadow war of the early years was conducted. Proving that the best fiction conveys reality better than most nonfiction, my old friend, soldier and explorer Wick Walker, begins to fill that gap with *Goat Game.*

Wick and I first met in Pakistan in the mid-1980s and have crossed paths regularly since. No one knows both sides of the Pak-Afghan Frontier as he does. He has climbed the mountains, run the rivers, and sipped tea in countless tribal councils. In these thirteen tales, he offers readers a boots-on-the-ground feel for life and operations in this topographically and culturally rugged region. Significantly and accurately, he depicts the complex relationship of three of the most fascinating and dangerous societies on the planet: the native Pushtuns, the intruding Arab fanatics that became al-Qa'ida, and the US Army Special Forces.

These were not the dramatic raids of today's Afghanistan, with armed drone aircraft circling overhead, high-tech communications equipment, armored vests, and heavy firepower. It was success not by brute force but rather through patience, courage, and a willingness to go into dangerous places where you depended on your knowledge, language skills, training, and personal relationships to survive. This was a cat-and-mouse game of making contact with your agents; gathering information; sitting around a smoking campfire drinking endless cups of hot, harsh tea with a tribal leader and his key lieutenants; and trying to read the situation through the nuances of body language and things not said. It was knowing that a friend of a month ago might now be an enemy, his loyalties having shifted for any number of reasons. It was huddling in a rough hillside dugout while Soviet 240mm rockets pounded around you, your presence in the area having been communicated by unseen observers. It was rarely a case of taking personal, direct action. Much more often it was like the passage in Wick's story "Sultan of Swat," when Bailey waits with Sultan and they hear volleys of rifle fire then two muted shots— mission accomplished.

Reading these tales I was continually impressed with how well Wick captures the feel of the tribal areas. The small villages, the dusty streets, the smell of smoky wood fires, the pace and cadence of conversations—this is the way it was. Enjoy these stories, for you are entering a world that has in many ways passed by, changed by the influx of technology, advanced weaponry, surveillance drones, precision-guided munitions, night-vision devices, and millions of dollars flooding into the hands of backward tribal peoples. The Afghan-Pak border area will only continue to change. These excellent tales—like Kipling's stories of British India—will serve to preserve that era when tribal warriors took on the Soviet Army in the mountains of Afghanistan and won.

Gary C. Schroen
Alexandria, Virginia, 2012

CIA veteran Gary Schroen was the Agency's Chief of Station for Afghanistan in the 1980s. Immediately following the World Trade Center attacks in 2001, he led the first team of Americans into Afghanistan to evict the Taliban and hunt down al-Qa'ida. He holds the Intelligence Cross, the highest award given by the CIA, and is the author of *First In: An Insider's Account of How the CIA Spearheaded the War on Terror in Afghanistan.*

GOAT GAME

A BORDER INCIDENT

*Before our eyes the sands of an expiring epoch are
fast running out; and the hour-glass of destiny is
once again being turned on its base.*

—The Honourable George Nathaniel Curzon, M.P.,
future Viceroy of India, at Bokhara observing the con-
solidation of Czarist dominion over Central Asia in 1888

NORTH-WEST FRONTIER PROVINCE, PAKISTAN, 1988

Hot from the bowels of a charcoal-fired brick oven at a roadside tea stand, the flat, unleavened bread smelled every bit
as good as Major Bailey had anticipated for the last three
hours. An orange sun, just appearing over the ridge behind them
and beginning to cut the cold of the desert night, didn't hurt of
course—nor did the spicy sense of the unknown ahead. He reached
across the dusty hood of the Land Cruiser, where the discs of bread
lay stacked on a newsprint place mat of yesterday's *Frontier Post,*

1

and tore off a sizable piece. His companion, Major Sultan, poured two cups full of sweet, milky tea from a chipped and battered blue enamel teapot. "Breakfast of Champions," Major Bailey intoned, hoisting the scalding tea in toast.

Although the two old friends had made dozens of similar trips over the last four years, through some of the remotest regions of Pakistan's North-West Frontier, Major Bailey had no idea of his companion's true name. Officers of Pakistan's Special Services Group worked in alias with foe and ally alike, and "Sultan" was just a "camp name." Well, so too was "Bailey." Both ranks of course were real; officers do not misrepresent themselves to one another under any circumstance.

It was hard to believe, but this might be nearly the last of their forays into the rugged and lawless tribal territory along the border between Pakistan and Afghanistan in search of examples of Soviet military technology unknown to the US and NATO. The headline that extended from beneath their bread read, "Soviets Might Withdraw Before Year's End, UN Envoy Declares." The trade in captured Soviet materiel, so lucrative to both Mujahedin fighters and Western intelligence, would soon dry up if this previously unthinkable abandonment of the Brezhnev Doctrine occurred.

That looming, if hypothetical, deadline lent urgency to their current mission. The warlord who had come forward this time, Bacha Khan, claimed to have a truck-mounted chemical warfare laboratory hidden in a cave. On his tribe's honor, he had sworn it was the long-sought key to the often rumored, never proven "yellow rain" said to have killed off the populations of entire valleys deep inside Afghanistan. In gratitude for the years of support from The Friends, Bacha Khan would part with his trophy for an even million dollars—a compact bundle that always seemed heavier than its actual twenty-three pounds: rubber-banded slabs of hundred-dollar bills, ten thousand dollars per slab, fitting inconspicuously into one of the small green canvas duffels the rug merchants in Islamabad gave away to their Western customers to transport their souvenirs.

Major Bailey believed none of this—not that the Red Army would retreat by year's end nor that the wily old Pushtun warrior had authentic chemical warfare equipment. With centuries of experience as smugglers, kidnappers, counterfeiters, and fabricators of sophisticated homemade weaponry, the border tribesmen had no equals in the extortive arts. Only with the guidance of the equally wily Major Sultan, himself a Pushtun, had Bailey been able to detect most, although by no means all, of the numerous attempts to sell him sinister-looking devices covered with Cyrillic writing that actually had originated in dusty Frontier workshops.

But if there was even the remotest chance that this could reveal a threat that Americans would face on the next battlefield, in the next war, then it must be investigated—even to the ends of the Earth, even to Waziristan.

They had left Pakistan's capital, Islamabad, the previous evening. Shortly after five p.m., recognized by Bailey's house guard, Sultan had pulled his blue Toyota without pause through the steel gates in the wall that surrounded the house and garden. When they departed a cup of tea later, no observer on the street could have told through the vehicle's dark-tinted windows how many occupants it held or of what nationalities. Over voluminous baggy trousers knotted around his waist with a cotton cord, Bailey wore a loose-fitting khaki shirt with tails that fell to his knees in front and back. Above his salt-and-pepper beard, a white skullcap covered most of his brown hair.

In the driver's seat, Sultan was similarly attired, although in his case shirt and trousers were pure white and topped with a light-weight, well-tailored black vest—hallmarks of the Pakistani upper class. On his wrist a steel Rolex with the palm and scimitars of Saudi Arabia on its face revealed a tour of duty in that country, although he never had explained to Major Bailey what particular mission had resulted in that mark of royal appreciation.

Major Sultan steered the vehicle rapidly along the wide, nearly deserted avenues of Islamabad. Then, upon rounding a traffic circle and passing one of the many police checkpoints that reserve the capital city for the governing elite, the two men plunged into the maelstrom of Rawalpindi traffic. Garish with bright murals of jet fighters and busty Indian film stars, overloaded Flying Coach buses surged through crowded streets, throwing off bow waves of scur-rying pedestrians, while schools of motorbikes and three-wheeled taxis darted in mysterious formations through the intersections. It was said in the diplomatic quarter that Pakistan began at the Islamabad city limits, and Bailey thought of the city as an island in the turbulent seas of Asia.

Arabist, explorer, and travel writer Dame Freya Stark wrote from Baghdad in 1938, "There is a delightful feeling of security about islands on a holiday, like being tucked up in bed; though it would be horrid to be a prisoner on one for long, security being blissful only in small doses." With its guard towers and spotlights glaring on razor-wired walls, the high-security American Embassy in Islamabad certainly resembled a prison. Perhaps Bailey was on work-release parole, speeding up the Grand Trunk Road toward Pakistan's legendary Frontier town of Peshawar. Or perhaps he was like Kim, on glorious summer holiday from the Raj boarding school in Lucknow, rushing to new adventures with his mentor, the red-bearded Pushtun horse trader Mahbub Ali.

It was dusk as they sped across the long bridge that spanned the braided channels and shifting sandbar islands of the Indus River, and full dark forty minutes later as they burrowed their way deep within the narrow alleyways of Peshawar to a small, walled compound they maintained in an Afghan refugee neighborhood. Around them the city seethed with a heady blend of danger, corruption, idealism, and despair unique to wartime capitols. Although every physical detail was different, the city reminded Bailey of Saigon in the early 1970s. Hundreds of thousands of Afghan refugees fleeing the violence in their homeland coexisted uneasily with their Pakistani kinsmen, while merchants, smugglers, moneychangers, and truckers from all of Asia jostled for the spoils of war.

Within these throngs, the Western community in Peshawar had a village quality. There were overwhelmed medical and aid workers from a dozen European and British Empire countries; diplomats, soldiers, and spies from throughout Europe and the Middle East; the hungry war correspondents who flocked like crows to every battlefield; and those who wanted to be taken for any one of the above. Periodically there were touring groups of safari-suited anticommunist zealots with flat American Midwestern accents, on pilgrimage to the land where the Cold War had turned hot—the "Banana Republicans." The transients rubbed shoulders in the lobbies of either the four-star Pearl Continental Hotel or the more economical Dean's, whose bungalows provided more ambiance but also more rodents. All—old Frontier hands and one-time gawkers alike—saw and were seen evenings at the American Club, a boon sponsored by the American Consulate and the only place in the Muslim town where Westerners could find cold beer.

Except, of course, for those who wished neither to see nor be seen. Bailey and Sultan rose at three in the morning, rolled quietly through the predawn streets of the city, and were far into the rugged barren lands to the south and west before Sultan pulled the Land Cruiser to a halt beside a stream to perform his ritual wash and morning prayer. After yet another hour, villages were awakening, and they could obtain the bread and milky tea they wolfed down over the dusty hood of their vehicle.

They rolled on through the morning, Bailey gripping the front edge of the passenger seat to hold his body down and stable in the lurching vehicle, feeling like a bull rider. Major Sultan broke the long companionable silence to announce that he had been selected to attend the Pakistani Army's staff college at Quetta; the next class would begin early in the New Year. Like its American counterpart, the Command and General Staff College at Fort Leavenworth, Kansas, this prestigious course groomed mid-level officers for higher levels of command and staff responsibilities. Selection was a mark of distinction and graduation a prerequisite for upward mobility. Most classes, Sultan pointed out, included one US Army officer, attending by invitation in lieu of training at Leavenworth. Could Bailey not volunteer, with his experience in the area giving him an advantage over other nominees?

With a wry smile, Bailey replied that his superiors already had counseled him to do no such thing. Special Operations duty often was regarded with suspicion, if not contempt, by the conventional brothers-in-arms of the American Infantry, Armor, and Field Artillery, and even within Special Forces detached duty such as Bailey's was met with a degree of skepticism. No troops were commanded, no voluminous staff studies or briefings were produced; it was difficult to define but clearly too much adventure and fun for a serious field grade officer. Major Bailey, who already had seen numbers of his contemporaries promoted to lieutenant colonel, with the foremost now commanding their own battalions, had best forsake running around the wilderness with his tribal friends and spend a tour or two back in the professional mainstream with his fellow officers on important staffs.

For the first time in almost twenty years, Bailey confided, he was entertaining vague thoughts of life out of uniform. His superiors were not wrong; there was something seductive, perhaps subversive, in spending too long among these rugged hills and their militantly independent inhabitants.

As Bailey launched into his explanation, a smile emerged on Major Sultan's face, and by its end a white-toothed grin split his dark countenance from ear to ear. With both irony and glee, he explained that his superiors had counseled him in much the same fashion. Except, they had no concern about him gadding about the wild Frontier, consorting with tribals from both sides of the border. What was seductive, and perhaps subversive, in their eyes (that an ambitious officer learned a bit about to his advantage but experienced too much at his peril), was American. The superpower's alluring ideals but fickle alliances, its personal freedom but decadent culture, and its unlimited power and funds would cast a pall over any foreign officer who spent too long within their orbit.

At noon they halted briefly at the mud-walled fortress of the Tochi Frontier Scouts, eating lunch with the commander while Major Sultan appraised him of their mission and arranged for them to stay the night at the officers' mess on their return journey. The two Pakistani officers conversed quietly in Urdu too rapid for Bailey to follow. A single mess orderly stood just outside the open doorway, within easy summons but unable to overhear the conversation, his khaki regimental uniform accented by a Tochi Scouts badge and red cockade in his tightly wound green turban.

From high on tall, whitewashed walls, trophy heads of Marco Polo sheep and ibex gazed down. Portraits of a century of former battalion commanders flanked the long banquet table and extended down the entrance hall, the older ones red-faced Englishmen, the more recent Pakistani, together an unbroken line of martial tradition and tribal warfare experience. In a corner stood an ornate bar of mahogany and brass, its display of whisky bottles banished for forty years, but its wood, brass, and crystal glasses gleaming with polish and respect.

A last few remnants of the Raj, and the Great Game, mused Bailey, *preserved in the desert air.*

Beside the bar hung a faded black-and-white photograph of a canvas-winged monoplane, the lanky figure of a Royal Air Force mechanic posed beside its open cockpit. From previous visits Major Bailey recognized the high forehead, beaked nose, and prominent chin of Airman Shaw, easily identified from the front piece portrait in *Seven Pillars of Wisdom.* As always, Bailey wondered which war had brought T.E. Lawrence all the way to Waziristan.

Two lurching hours later, Bailey and Sultan pulled off the road behind a parked Nissan truck, so caked with dirt its faded red paint was almost indistinguishable, where a dry riverbed, or *nullah*, debouched from the rugged hills on their left to intersect the road. Three black-eyed Afghans unblinkingly regarded them from the truck bed, assault rifles and grenade launchers slung across their backs, ammunition belts crisscrossing their chests, the tails of their turbans pulled across their lower faces to protection from sun and dust. After a short conference with the two occupants in the cab, Sultan returned to his driver's seat, and they picked their way slowly up the *nullah* behind the other vehicle, their windows now rolled up to avoid the choking clouds of dust raised by the truck ahead.

Without stopping they passed a small mud-and-brick mosque, its minaret painted a faded green, and a half-dozen single-story buildings clustered among a scattering of trees, a natural spring or oasis in the otherwise barren landscape. Knowing from experience where to look, Major Bailey spotted sentries high on the ridges that overlooked the site, and the signature long-barreled profile of a "Dishka" antiaircraft gun. Bacha Khan, Major Sultan had learned from their guides, was not presently available. His deputies would lead them directly to where the captured truck was stored; they would speak with the warlord later, on the way back down.

The rutted trail led farther up the *nullah*, and the sides of the ravine became more vertical. They passed the black mouths of several "caves"—tunnels blasted horizontally deep into the mountainside, their entrances smoothed and reinforced with brick arches, safe havens from bombardment. Finally the lead truck pulled to a halt where the ruts outlined a crude turnaround. A chinar tree with pale dusty leaves, cousin to the American sycamore, shaded the small flat area, in the center of which stood a single Muslim grave, unadorned flat rocks at head and foot, a slim vertical pole and green banner identifying a martyr of the holy war against the Russians. A foot track continued up a steep slope to their right to another tunnel entrance. The two majors dismounted their vehicle and hiked eagerly toward their objective, walking a relief after the punishing drive, as their escorts squatted patiently in the sparse shade by the grave.

A raised voice from the direction of the cave, an unfamiliar accent distinctly not the Pushtu he was so used to hearing, if not fully understanding, caused Bailey to glance up sharply while simultaneously sliding his hand inside the open top of his camera bag to grip the 9mm Makarov that fit so nicely in the slot for a 50mm lens. After the invasion in '79, this regulation sidearm for Soviet officers quickly had become both status symbol and badge of rank for Afghan Mujahedin commanders, and Bailey was not above indulging in the same vanity, albeit concealed.

As a tall—very tall—black man emerged from the hard shadow of the cave's mouth, Bailey's first instinct was one of relief and recognition of a fellow countryman, for in this part of the world almost all of the blacks he encountered were Americans, either State Department or Marine Guard Detachment. Almost as quickly, however, he was disillusioned by the ugly long-barreled Soviet PK machine gun suspended from a strap around the figure's neck and trained purposefully in their direction. A long white cotton robe falling straight to the ankles, with an equally white, small turban, looked Sudanese or Somali, and every inch of the figure's perhaps six-and-a-half feet vibrated with hostility.

To Bailey's left Sultan stood immobile, surveying the incongruous scene, feet slightly spread and right hand thrust deep within the waist-level slash pocket of his long shirt. Behind them the Nissan pickup that had led them from camp headquarters to the caves roared to life and sped back down the dirt track. The two majors silently exchanged glances. To Bailey's raised-eyebrow query—"Is this a setup?"—Sultan's shrug replied, "I can't tell yet."

Tearing his attention away from the figure in front of them, Bailey noted that the three Mujahedin escorts who had ridden up the hill in the back of the Nissan remained squatting in the shadow of the chinar tree, weapons still slung across their backs. Their casual posture was reassuring, but the black-bearded Afghans did not return his look. All focused instead a few hundred meters farther up the draw, where a cluster of white canvas tents stood, blue

UNHCR initials across their flanks. From the nearest emerged four men, double-timing down the draw in their direction.

The four wore light-colored Afghan shirts and trousers, with white skullcaps on their heads as favored by many Afghans in the summer heat, but even at a distance they appeared subtly different from the Mujahedin lounging under the chinar. They wore no vests over their shirts, and while most sported black mustaches, their beards were either incipient or absent, revealing pale fleshy cheeks that would have been incongruous on Afghan fighters. Three carried Kalashnikov assault rifles, and slung across their chests were green canvas pouches containing extra magazines. In the lead hurried a thin man, smooth-shaven with Arabic features, armed only with a black, brick-shaped walkie-talkie.

"Wahabbi," muttered Sultan in a low voice only his companion could hear, inflecting the single word with both scorn and wariness, as if describing a scorpion. He used the term not as in Saudi Arabia to denote the particular, conservative sect of Islam to which the House of Saud belonged but rather as it was used throughout South Asia—as a pejorative and generic label for Islamic militants, most of them Arabs. Xenophobic, fanatic, suicidal—in the wake of the invasion by Soviet atheists, hundreds had swarmed to Afghanistan, ostensibly to aid their fellow Muslims but in fact on their own dark quest for martyrdom.

The pragmatic Afghans took the huge sums of money with which the wahabbis were provided by Islamic "charities," armed them to the teeth, and sent them off like unguided missiles to harass Red Army positions, and die. Otherwise the Afghans preferred to have nothing to do with them. It was said on the streets of Peshawar that more Afghans than Soviets had died at the hands of the wahabbis; their death wish and total disregard for tactical security drew enemy fire on one and all, and their attempts to proselytize the Muslim but fiercely libertarian Afghans to their own fanatic cults frequently led to gunfire.

Breathless, the blue-clad leader halted directly in front of Major Sultan. He neither responded to Bailey's universal Arabic greeting, *salaamalaykum,* nor acknowledged the American's presence with even a glance from his narrow-set onyx eyes. A head shorter than Sultan's five feet ten inches and half the burly Special Service Group officer's bulk, he shifted his weight from foot to foot in agitation as he launched into a lengthy diatribe, punctuated by forceful gestures with the radio antenna, like a bantam-weight boxer taunting a heavyweight.

Engage, engage, engage! rang like a mantra in the back of Major Bailey's consciousness. *While they're talking, they're not doing something worse.* The advice, from a long-ago hostage negotiation course, offered an alternative to the unblinking muzzle of the PK and perhaps a chance to buy some time to figure out what was happening here. Jumping assertively into a brief silence when the ranting figure paused for breath, Bailey addressed Sultan, "Translate like we're in a meeting. Include me here. What's he going on about? Tell him we're friends of Bacha Khan."

"He says this is sacred ground, a jihad. They will die here. Infidels should not be here," Major Sultan briefed rapidly.

"Tell him all the People of the Book support this jihad; we all are helping in different ways. The world must know about this holy

13

struggle," intoned Bailey, as he nodded politely toward the Arab, who still pointedly stared only at Sultan.

Major Sultan's next, measured comments provoked another long flurry of staccato Arabic, during which Bailey puzzled over what might have led to this confrontation. Had the Pushtun warlord simply forgotten that wahabbis were bivouacked in this *nullah*, or had he misjudged their volatility? Or was it not entirely by accident that Bailey and Sultan were confronted by their only possible rivals with ample motive and funds for the purchase of chemical warfare equipment? Perhaps a scheme not only to provoke a bidding war (which he could have done down at his headquarters) but also to pressure Bailey into putting down cash without a careful look at the equipment?

If so, Bacha Khan was playing a dangerous game—for Majors Bailey and Sultan, of course, but also for himself. The Pakistanis and their American allies were not just customers for occasional sales of captured Soviet items, but the pipeline for all the ammunition and materiel that underwrote the war, one of the twin foundations of any warlord's power and prestige. The other foundation of tribal power was more subtle, but even more dominant: *pushtunwali,* the code of the Pushtuns, the code of honor that governs every aspect of Frontier life. At the very core of *pushtunwali* lay the absolute protection of guests at the tribal hearth. For centuries, tribesmen had fought to the death to repel invaders and to defend guests while on tribal lands, regardless of the visitors' transgressions elsewhere. Any leader who did not uphold this tenet of tribal honor would instantly lose the moral authority by which he dominated his unruly tribesmen; there was never a shortage of cousins and nephews ready to pounce if a leader's grip should slip.

To date, both of these factors of tribal power had allowed the two majors to travel the Frontier in relative safety, and Major Bailey's instinct was not to back down now in the face of this assault from outsiders. In his experience, signs of weakness and willingness to compromise seldom led to good outcomes in Asia. At his side he sensed a similar steel in his companion's posture and tone of voice.

Times of change, however, are always dangerous. Throughout Afghanistan, long-bearded, black-eyed men watched from the mountains for the impending retreat of the Red Army, and it was not peace they looked forward to. Warlords hoarded money and ammunition, forged new alliances and enmities, prepared for the gathering contest for the throne in Kabul. Bailey wondered what risks Bacha Khan was willing to undertake.

The answer arrived in the lanky form of the man himself. Three vehicles sped up to the flat below: their original escort, a similar, equally battered Toyota Hilux, and the warlord's metallic-blue Mitsubishi SUV. A dozen Mujahedin sprang from the backs of the trucks, none less than six feet tall, none armed with less than a Kalashnikov with extra magazines and hand grenades, several sporting fully loaded rocket-propelled grenade launchers as well. *Allah too*, thought Bailey, *is on the side of the heaviest battalions.*

Descending from the driver's seat of the Mitsubishi, Bacha Khan strode rapidly up the slope toward Bailey, Sultan, and the mouth of the cave. An elaborate white-and-black turban surmounted his sun-and-wind-etched face, and a long curly beard, henna-dyed to a burnt orange, fell across his chest. From right shoulder to left hip crossed a leather bandoleer studded with 9mm cartridges, from which hung the perquisite Makarov pistol.

At his shoulder trailed his eldest son, a thin boy of twelve dressed in khaki, with leather sandals, a soiled red-and-gold pillbox cap, and a Spetsnaz model AK-74 assault rifle with folding stock and brick-red magazine. Major Bailey had never seen the warlord without his son. The boy served tea and food to honored guests, sat silently in the back corner of councils of war, spoke only when addressed, and daily absorbed the unfathomable nuances of wielding power as a border chieftain.

Bailey smoothly removed his right hand from his camera bag and placed it over his heart in the traditional gesture of peace and friendship, then stepped a pace toward the approaching pair. Next to him, Sultan also removed his hand from his waistband. Less wisely, the tall Sudanese continued to level his machine gun in their direction, provoking an angry tirade from the warlord directed to the skinny Arab. With a sullen look, the Arab gestured to his minion to avert the muzzle.

After another salvo of Arabic from the warlord, the Arab abruptly about-faced and stalked off stiff-backed toward the tents, trailed by his several companions. Halfway to the bivouac site, the small group halted in animated but inaudible discussion, then squatted in the shade of a large boulder, silently watching the men at the cave's mouth and the Afghans by the vehicles. Bacha Khan addressed Major Sultan briefly in Pushtu. "This is not a good situation," Sultan summarized. "He wants to talk further at his headquarters below. He has tea and dinner prepared." Bacha Khan and his son already were turning toward their return path as Sultan spoke.

Sultan's hint of a smile and ironic tone communicated the subtext privately to Bailey. This haste to return down the *nullah*, without even seeing the "yellow rain truck" not more than a fifty meters from where they stood, and the readiness of a dinner feast that both knew would have required hours for the women to prepare, reinforced all of their previous suspicions. As much as tribal leaders were revered for protecting their guests from harm, so too were they admired for relieving them of their purses.

Regardless of the Pushtun's infuriating ploys, Bailey knew he could neither get approval to buy the mysterious truck without verifying its authenticity nor in conscience abandon it to the crouching figures watching them from up the *nullah* without confirming it to be a fake.

"Tell him how honored we are to accept his invitation. Also tell him it won't take us more than five minutes to take the pictures of the chemical truck that Washington requires," Bailey responded, fitting the flash attachment to his bulky Canon and striding toward the entrance to the tunnel before the warlord could respond.

"As *Wash-ing-ton* wills," Bacha Khan relented, seemingly at a loss for further reasons that might dissuade the inscrutable *Wash-ing-ton*. He made no move to accompany them into the cave, however. If it did turn out to be a fake, Bailey was sure the warlord would want to say he hadn't actually seen it himself. Bailey wondered how one said "plausible deniability" in Pushtu.

It required only moments inside the dark tunnel to confirm their suspicions. The Cyrillic writing on the bumper of the truck identified the "chemical weapons laboratory" as a component of a Soviet mobile field hospital, and a glance inside revealed nothing but a centrifuge and other apparatus for routine blood testing. Typically, the Soviet medical equipment appeared generations older than similar units that served the Mujahedin from Médecins Sans Frontières, Red Crescent, and others. As the two majors exited the cave and remounted their vehicle to convoy down the draw, the five squatting figures remained immobile in the shadow of the boulder above.

The game of course had to be played out to its logical and face-saving end. Over mounds of saffron rice and joints of lamb torn into bite-size pieces by greasy fingers, Major Bailey thanked Bacha Khan for his extraordinary hospitality and for notifying them of his remarkable trophy. The two rolls of film and a detailed report would be transmitted the very next day to experts in Washington, who were eagerly standing by to determine what it was and how much it might be worth. And of course if Bacha Khan obtained anything else of interest, Washington was always in the market.

When Sultan finally steered out of the *nullah* and up onto the dirt road that led back toward the Tochi Scouts' fortress, the two men exchanged glances and tightlipped smiles, then retreated into separate reveries. To the pounding of the Land Cruiser's stiff suspension, Bailey felt the muscles in his neck and shoulders slowly unknot, the metallic taste of adrenaline recede, the tunnel vision and laser focus of the battlefield broaden like the widening of a zoom lens.

It was the last hour of daylight, *hawa khana*, the time of "breathing the air," before the two friends spoke of their encounter. They sat on rattan armchairs on a lush grass courtyard outside the Tochi Scouts officers' mess. Bougainvillea trailed a crimson curtain over the whitewashed compound wall, its sweet, heavy scent contrasting with the acrid smell of evening cook fires from the town. In the surrounding rocky hills, jackals exchanged high-pitched howls as they gathered into packs to scavenge the town dumps and alleys after dark.

"If Allah wills," began Sultan thoughtfully, "perhaps these remote valleys are now witnessing the final battles of the world's most recent clash of empires and ideologies, as they have so many times before. Is it possible that today we saw the emergence of the next?"

Bailey glanced around the fortress and the darkening hills beyond. "Since before the tales of Homer, the end of one war has sown the dragon's teeth of the next. But who can know which ones will sprout or when and which will be tomorrow's enemy or ally? At least for now, for a little while, *sufficient unto the day is the evil thereof.*"

THE EUNUCH OF 'PINDI

A stone's throw out on either hand
From that well-ordered road we tread,
And all the world is wild and strange....

For we have reached the Oldest Land
Wherein the Powers of Darkness range.

—Rudyard Kipling,
"From the Dusk to the Dawn"

ISLAMABAD, PAKISTAN, 1990

For days a ragged cavalcade flowed past the Diplomatic Quarter, turned before the Parliament buildings, and spilled into the vacant land between the capital and the Islamic University campus. Motor coaches, rooftops piled high with luggage, bore license plates from Karachi, Multan, Lahore, and a dozen other cities across the Punjab and the Sind. Brightly painted

21

Flying Coach buses, their ornate tin filigree luggage racks imitating the platforms atop Mogul elephants, pulsed with horn and drum. Sturdy farm tractors hung with tinsel and garlands of plastic flowers pulled trailers packed standing room only with singing, flag-waving humanity. Caravans of camels, rarely allowed in the capital city, marched in ungainly but stately files down the highway shoulder, proudly swinging bells and red wool tassels. The black-windowed motorcades of ministers and diplomats yielded right of way.

Out on the flat, barely visible from the higher rooftops of the embassies, where a rocky buttress from the khaki Margalla Hills met the plain, grew day by day a sprawling tent city, laid out not by municipal planners but by centuries of custom. The annual festival at the shrine of the great Sufi saint, Imam Bari, was getting underway.

At the end of a teeming parking area, Major Bailey stretched his cramped legs while Major Sultan paid the driver of their tiny white-and-yellow taxi. The distant Islamabad skyline shimmered like a mirage in the hot dusty sunshine, and little dust devils chased across the plain. Probably dust *dervishes* here, Bailey decided. To the north, bright white thunderheads towered above the hills. He briefly wished he had brought his daypack with rain jacket, water bottle, and camera. But pilgrims don't wear GORE-TEX. Both men wore the ubiquitous *shalwar kameez* (baggy trousers and cotton shirt with tails falling to the knees), dusty sandals on their feet, white skullcaps on their heads.

The two friends launched themselves onto a crowded footpath and allowed the current of humanity to sweep them into the labyrinth. Their route was walled with shouting vendors, pushcarts laden with pyramids of fresh oranges, pomegranates, and mangos; syrupy drinks; candies hard and soft; scarves in hundreds of vivid patterns. Fragrant barbecue stands offered *charpoy* rope beds to sit for a moment and escape the crowd, hot sausages, and tin cups of cold, refreshing, lethal water. Over everything hung a uniquely South Asian musk of dust, wood smoke, curry, and hashish.

Even Major Sultan seemed to pick up the holiday spirit. Bailey never had seen the serious, often pugnacious Special Services Group officer so smiling and animated. There was even perhaps a play-fulness about him, as if he were keeping some secret or surprise from his friend. They paused while Sultan bought candy—gelat-inous ropey strands that resembled translucent amber spaghetti, scooped into a fold of torn newspaper. Offering some to Bailey, Sultan explained, "You won't like it. I don't even like it myself. It is too sweet, but when I was a child, my father would get this for me at the Eid celebrations and all the festivals. So now I dislike the taste, but I love the memories it brings."

Cotton candy stuck all over your hands and face, thought Bailey, *and fighting yellow jackets for your Coke and corn dog at sweltering county fairs each summer. Been there.*

Nearer the shrine and mosque, commercial vendors gave way to fakirs selling religious and magical talismans from shady perches on the roots of banyan trees. Clad in an eye-catching variety of loin-cloths, chains, ashes, beards, and tattoos, and enveloped in clouds of blue hemp smoke, they drew enthusiastic, laughing crowds with antics and exhortations incomprehensible to Major Bailey.

At the hub, by the front and sides of the mosque and shrine, rectangles had been roped off into dusty stages. Dueling bands of drums, flutes, and oddly shaped stringed instruments competed for attention while male dancers skipped and spun in brightly wrought tribal finery. A dun camel swayed and bowed in time to its owner's drum. In the background, Major Bailey recognized the gypsy and his dancing bear that camped along the airport road, both now sporting ornate embroidered vests. Raucous crowds clapped and stomped to the music, showering exceptional performers with small rupee notes and coins.

Suddenly a blast of wind raced through, powerful enough to rip loose plastic canopies from merchants' stalls and send them careening after panicked donkeys and camels. Thunderheads obscured the sun, and a curtain of rain and hail swept down from the hills. Merchants and performers leapt to pack and shelter their goods, while thousands of onlookers ran for shelters, illuminated by seemingly continuous sheets of lightning. Waves of thunder rolled one upon the next.

Without hesitation, Major Sultan seized Bailey's elbow and steered them both down a wide set of stairs and under the mosque, only Sultan's linebacker's bulk and forceful grip getting the two through the stampeding mob and under the protected overhang un-separated. Taking his cue from his friend, Bailey slipped off his sandals, but instead of placing them in the rapidly growing pile of footgear at the foot of the steps, both men slipped them into the waistbands of their trousers.

Barefoot, they worked their way around the long, shallow pool for ablutions to the shadowed back of the chamber. A narrow doorway revealed a stone stairway upward to ground level, where Major Sultan plunged at full run back into the storm. Half-blinded by the pelting rain and hail, Bailey followed, across a muddy courtyard and through a gateway in the wall that surrounded the mosque. Soaked to the skin, the two dove into the open doorway of a low building that adjoined the wall, and were greeted by a blast of heat and sound. Incense hung like a curtain in the humid air.

At the far end of the room, two men played rhythmic, pounding music on drum and flute, while on the carpeted center floor a single figure swayed and danced in time. It was the same spinning, leaping dance as the ones performed outside, before the storm—yet totally different. With a shock, Bailey realized that this dancer was female, and young, her every movement sensual. Silver bracelets rattled in time to the music on slender ankles and wrists; indigo silk concealed and yet revealed a lithe figure. A crescent of black hair fell across her face, framing one dark long-lashed eye.

As the storm outside roared to a crescendo, the drums seemed to pick up the tempo of the thunder, and the dancer to whirl in time to the blazing lightning. She flowed across the carpet and halted, her back to the two officers, then sank to her knees. Arching her back, she gracefully extended her arms over her head. Then very slowly she leaned backward until her shoulders touched the carpet and her open palms lay just in front of the two officers. Tongue flicking to moisten glossy lips, she gazed up at them with unblinking, dilated eyes. Bailey suddenly noticed the pounding of rain on the tin roof and realized that both the music and the thunder were silent.

"Do not react in any way," whispered Sultan. With a barely suppressed chuckle, he added, "Remember, we are in the mysterious East, and things are seldom as they seem." Slowly he unfolded a crisp, one-thousand-rupee banknote and bent over to place it on the supine dancer's outstretched palms.

From nowhere an older woman appeared beside them, matronly, well groomed, necklace and earrings heavy with gold. Wordlessly she waved a hand to dismiss both band and dancer and escorted the two officers to chairs in a corner of the now deserted chamber. Beneath finely plucked eyebrows, her piercing black eyes fixed on Bailey. As Sultan translated, she began to speak in a disconcerting baritone, "I am called 'The Eunuch of 'Pindi,' and I am the nineteenth guru of the colony of *hijras*, or eunuchs, in Rawalpindi. The dancer you saw is my newest *chelas*, my acolyte. She dances at wedding parties and makes people happy and brings good fortune. We are the heirs of an ancient tradition that came to here from Turkistan, from a time when eunuchs administered the Celestial Empire of China, guarded the palaces and harems of Constantinople, sang the holy music of Rome. But that was long ago. Now we are the lowest caste, the invisibles, the Dust of Asia.

"What have such as we to do with an officer from the empire that now rules the world, more powerful than the Moghuls or the British Raj? To the northwest, in Afghanistan where the warlords killed the Russians and now they kill each other, an old evil is gathering its power. We have seen this fanatic sect wax and wane through the centuries, emerging from the Arabian Desert in the aftermath of tyranny and wars, pretending to bring justice and peace in the name of Islam, actually a cult of intolerance and death of innocents. It is the very opposite of the wondrous medley of South Asia, where Hindus, Muslims, Sikhs, Jains, and Christians mingle; where men of all castes and tribes and degrees of wealth share the sun and the monsoon rains and the red clay and the teeming cities. But it is your power they truly hate and fear, and they will attack by stealth, directly at the centers of your wealth and pride.

"However, that is not why I asked our friend to bring you here. We are fated never to be believed when we foretell bad news, and never to be thanked for the warning when it comes true. Now I would speak to you of more useful things—of a man departing Jalalabad in Afghanistan with a dangerous weapon and of a tea seller in the arms bazaar at Dara Adam Khel who knows his route and destination..."

Windows open to embrace the sweet clean evening air after the thunderstorms, the two majors drove down the wide, nearly deserted avenues of Islamabad. "Well," began Bailey, "thanks for a fascinating afternoon ... But, how much of that can we believe?"

"Many of our intelligence officers think that only the powerful elites have knowledge of important affairs," replied Sultan. "But I believe that groups on the very bottom rungs of society, those most threatened by every tremor in the social fabric, have ancient survival mechanisms, sources of information and means of communication long lost by those more privileged and protected. Like the Shi'a Hazaras in Afghanistan, or the ancient Nestorian Christians here—immigrants from the time of Constantine—or sometimes even the Sufis.

"Everywhere it is the *hijras*. Some say because the gods have deprived them of that which is most human, they have given them in compensation the ability to cast spells, of good or evil, and to foresee the future. Others say they are just a vicious sect of extortionists, that they roam the markets in packs, and if a merchant does not pay them to move on, they drive off his customers with vulgar behavior. It is even said that if they are not invited to bless and dance at a wedding—and well paid for it—the firstborn son may be stolen and inducted into their society.

"Whatever they are, one thing is certain. Everywhere the wahabbis succeed in establishing their Caliphate of Shaitan, they will kill off the *hijras* like pariah dogs, declaring them unclean. So as unlikely as it seems, they are our natural allies. And allies who are invisible, as the guru said, can be very valuable.

"Besides," Major Sultan added with an enigmatic grin, "it is said to be *very* bad luck to ignore these people."

NORTH-WEST PASSAGE

Don't ever march home the same way. Take a different route so you won't be ambushed.

—Rules of Rogers' Rangers, French and Indian War, 1757

NORTH-WEST FRONTIER PROVINCE, PAKISTAN, 1990

*J*ust *like driving to the firing ranges at Fort Bragg*, thought Major Bailey. They could hear the marketplace at Dara Adam Khel before it came into view ahead on the dusty road: rapid bursts of small arms fire, mostly on full automatic; the measured pops of pistols; and occasionally the whoosh and crump of a rocket-propelled grenade.

Set back to either side from the rutted road, high mud walls—blank but for locked, double metal gates wide enough to pass Bedford cargo trucks—surrounded huge invisible compounds. These were the famed gun factories of Dara, where a century before the rebellious tribesmen, denied modern weaponry by the British Raj, had learned to copy captured weapons and where today virtually any light or medium weapon in the world could be obtained in knockoff form. Here too would be warehouses of opium, hashish, and contraband of every sort. By tradition and treaty, in the tribal-areas trade, taxation and even most law enforcement were matters for tribal law and custom, and it was acknowledged by all that the government writ extended no more than a rifle shot from either side of the road.

Major Sultan chanted to himself in a low voice as he swung the Land Cruiser back and forth between potholes. Most of the Pushtu words were unfamiliar to Bailey, but he could recognize a regular cadence and rhyme. "Ah ha," he teased Sultan, "I always suspected you were a warrior poet."

"Sadly, not I," his friend responded with a grin, "at least not yet. That was by the most famous of all Pushtun warrior poets, Khushal Khan Khattak, about three centuries ago. It's archaic and difficult to translate of course, but part of it goes:

The Adam Khel Afridi maids
Are both rosy and fair;
Among them there are many beauties
With every kind of charm

With great bright eyes, long curling lashes
And eyebrows arched and wide,
With honey lips and rosy cheeks
And foreheads like the moon....

I came into Tirah county
Among the Adam Khels;

Now, sad at heart, I've taken leave
Of all these gentle souls."

"Warrior poets must travel in different circles than you and I,"
commented Bailey. "I've never seen such a collection of scoundrels
in my life as in this arms bazaar...zero pretty girls or gentle souls."

The bazaar itself appeared much the same as others in the region,
although larger and more prosperous. For about two hundred yards,
small shops lined both sides of the unpaved street, glass-fronted to
display their wares by day, steel-shuttered and padlocked during
prayers and at night. At intervals, shadowy shoulder-width alleyways led between the shop fronts to mysterious warehouse godowns
in the rear. Unique to Dara, however, was the barren hillside west
of the road and shops, which sloped upward to a boulder-crenu-
lated skyline, devoid of life. Absent were the usual goats, sheep,
and shepherd boys, even the ubiquitous gray-headed crows. This
was the impact area, where the shoppers directed the muzzles of the
weapons they were testing in front of the shops, where the rounds
fell harmlessly—unless, of course, the homemade weapon misfired
or exploded in the center of the crowded street. *Perhaps*, thought
Bailey, *that's why customers must pay cash in advance for their test ammunition, dollars or rupees only.*

On their left, as the two officers entered the marketplace,
stood a small pharmacy, windows flush with pill bottles and medical appliances. Incongruously, beside its narrow doorway hung a
bedraggled black goat pelt. For generations, lashed securely inside
such hides, bails of opium gum had come down from the hills with
the camel trains, until the black hide became the symbol across the

tribal areas of opium and hashish for sale. Directly opposite, just as described by the Eunuch of 'Pindi, Major Bailey noted a tea stall, its proprietor squatting motionless behind an enormous samovar of burnished copper, alert to every activity on the busy street.

Threading their way politely through the heavily armed pedestrian traffic, they drove to the far end of the bazaar and parked their SUV. Afoot they joined the milling shoppers, peering in windows, occasionally entering a shop to admire an old weapon or the very latest in German automatic carbines, haggling good naturedly over the prices of Soviet bayonets and red-star belt buckles. Gradually Bailey acquired enough souvenirs to satisfy visitors from Washington for the next several months.

Major Sultan settled on two Makarov pistols, new and shiny with cosmoline, just as they had come from corrupt Red Army quartermasters in Kabul. By the time they were presented to VIPs at the Special Services Group headquarters, Bailey knew, they would be battle scarred and pried from the cold, dead fingers of Russian officers. Perhaps the holsters and pistol belts would be dark with dried goat blood, like thousands of bullet-torn Viet Cong battle flags brought back from Vietnam by American soldiers, products of a thriving cottage industry established by the 5th Special Forces Group in the tribal camps and villages of Vietnam's central highlands.

Their reason for being in Dara demonstrated for all to see, and their allotted role in the economic life of the North-West Frontier fulfilled, the two officers sank gratefully onto a low bench in front of the tea stall. Savoring the surge of warmth and energy from the almost scalding combination of black tea, hot milk, and sugar, they observed the street to make sure no one approached to overhear as Major Sultan translated the low voice that spoke from behind the samovar.

"Peace be with you, *Sahibs*. The Guru requested it, so I will tell you what I have heard, although I do not know all of the story, or what it may mean. It is told here that last month, along the route between Parachinar, in Kurram Agency, and Ali Khel, in Afghanistan, a blood feud began between some wahabbis and the Mujahedin.

"Now, the wahabbis come here to fight the Russians, which is a good and holy thing, so we welcome them as our brothers. But many of them believe that because they come from the Land of the Two Mosques and the place of the Haj, they know better than we do how to worship Allah and practice Islam, and that part of their holy duty here is to teach us that our tribal elders and our *mullahs* are in error. So I must tell you what occurred on the way to Ali Khel.

"At the place where the track divides, and one way crosses the river toward Khost, and the other turns north into the Shining Mountains, where the nomad Chamkani caravans go up in the springtime, there are the graves of many Mujahedin who were martyred in the great victory over the Russians at Ali Khel two years ago. As is our way, the graves of those holy martyrs are marked with green flags, just as the graves of saints are decorated on their holy days.

"And on that day last month, a group of Mujahedin, Mangal tribesmen, discovered wahabbis tearing down those flags and throwing them on the ground and kicking over the headstones, because the wahabbis preach that placing of flags on graves, even holy ones, is *haram*, forbidden. The Mangals killed two of those destroying the graves, but four others escaped. Later it was learned that the leader of those wahabbis pronounced a *fatwa* against the Mangals.

"Perhaps you sahibs have heard this already in the Storytellers Bazaar in Peshawar. It is well known.

"But now it is also whispered that the wahabbis have a new weapon, a way to send captured Russian explosives to kill the Mangal leaders, and that the tribal *lashkar*, militia, cannot protect them, even inside the big refugee camp that now stands where the Chamkani once camped with their camel herds at the end of summer, just east of Parachinar. Perhaps it is like the wonderful eye-of-Allah that finds the Russian helicopter gunships when the *rocketwallas* fire their American missiles into the air.

"Perhaps you *sahibs* too are interested in this new weapon? It may be that a man departed Jalalabad with it yesterday and will be in Parachinar before the Friday prayers tomorrow."

Majors Bailey and Sultan rose to stretch their legs and make their way back to the vehicle for the punishing drive ahead. "May you never be weary," Sultan murmured, unobtrusively passing a large stack of rupee notes behind the samovar as he paid for their tea.

"May you never be poor," replied the soft voice from behind the urn.

A funeral procession wound through the bazaar in Parachinar, from the white-tented refugee camp to the east, heading toward a burial ground under the cliffs north of town. Like skeletal coffins, four rope *charpoy* beds, legs in the air so the bearers could get their shoulders beneath the frames, bore four bodies wrapped tightly in white cotton winding sheets. Behind, on a similarly inverted small wooden table, lay a white, child-size form. From the vantage point of a sentry tower at one corner of the Frontier Scouts garrison, Majors Bailey and Sultan, standing with post commander Lieutenant Colonel Malik, heard the incessant high pitched ululations of the women, punctuated by angry bursts of automatic weapons fire into the air from the crowds of men accompanying the bodies.

Colonel Malik filled in the just-arrived majors. "Most say that the bomber must have been an Arab, a wahabbi. Thousands and thousands of Mujahedin suffered terrible hardships, took incredible risks, and died by the Russian guns, rockets, and mines. Disease killed thousands more among the millions in the refugee camps. But not one ever took his own life. To die along with your enemy is not satisfactory *badal,* revenge. Besides, suicide is *haram,* forbidden, in Islam as in Christianity. Others, though, say it was an Afridi boy from a village in the Tirah Valley, too simple to go to school so he herded the village goats, who fell under the spell of an Egyptian wahabbi named Rashid. That is why no one noticed when a stranger joined the men at the mosque, wearing explosives covered with nails under his blanket.

"In any case, the tribes are incensed—not just the Mangals and other Sunni tribes, but the usually quiet but fierce Shi'a, even the aloof nomads. It is not a good time to be a stranger anywhere in the Kurram Valley, and I do not believe you'll learn anything more from here. Of the bomber, only the legs remain. And, strangely, the face and scalp; all the skin above the neck peeled off the skull as neatly as the tiger head mounted over the fireplace in the billiard room of our officers' mess. In the *hadith*, the Prophet—Peace Be Upon Him—teaches us that a suicide will forever suffer in hell the same death he inflicted upon himself. I am a professional soldier, and I live with the deaths of both enemies and friends—but I will have nightmares of that faceless, eternally howling creature.

"This much I think is now clear. The new weapon you were warned of is not a missile guidance system. I pray this was a single, deranged individual, but I fear the wahabbis have learned to enslave reason and religion, and steer men like robots even to certain death and hellfire."

Major Sultan nodded thoughtfully. "After our race to get here, we were both looking forward to a restful evening in the mess, with you and your officers and your tiger. But travel to Parachinar is always easier and safer than returning, because there's no alternative to retracing the route down the single long road along the valley. Now it would be best to travel faster than the rumor of our presence—if that is possible."

Through the long afternoon, their little convoy wound its way back toward the settlements of Pakistan—Majors Sultan and Bailey in their blue Land Cruiser, a following white Mitsubishi with six plainclothes riflemen behind its darkened windows, and a nondescript red-and-gray Hilux truck driven by two turbaned tribesmen who leapfrogged the others, sometimes far ahead, sometimes stopping for tea or prayer and falling behind, never obviously accompanying the other vehicles. By day, even in quiet times, the route was a gauntlet of armed, blood-feuding tribesmen, Afghan Mujahedin passing through to the front lines against the Soviets, drug and gun traffickers, all under the dubious policing of the Frontier Scouts militia. By night, Bailey knew, it became a complete no man's land.

At one point three gunshots rang out from a nearby hillock as they passed, deliberate and evenly spaced. No harm came to either vehicle, but Major Sultan immediately braked and pulled the Land Cruiser to a dusty halt on the left shoulder of the road. Extending his arm and pistol out the driver's window, he snapped off two shots in quick succession then let out the clutch to resume their journey. Nothing more transpired, yet Bailey was quite sure that had they not slowed and responded to the implied challenge, one or more trucks full of armed tribesmen would have raced down to the road to investigate the strangers. "Unarmed, you are my enemy" was more than a casual Pushtun expression.

After a final rest break at a busy roadside tea stall, as the sun set behind them, a noticeably more alert and concerned Major Sultan resumed his place behind the wheel. His roving, low-profile escort had identified a dusty pickup and two heavily bearded occupants who showed an unwholesome curiosity about the two SUVs. For the last hour-and-a-half, they had followed at a considerable distance, then sped ahead, only to stop out of sight until Bailey and

Sultan passed, to pick up the trail once again. "Angry hornets from the Mangal nest? Ordinary bandits? Or could we even have been lured out here for some purpose?" mused Sultan. "Whatever they are, do they have other, so far unidentified allies? I think it is time, as our brothers in the infantry say, to 'break contact.' "

Sultan had allies of his own, it turned out. As dusk fell, and the danger of bandit gangs preying on passersby became acute, the rare police posts blocked the highway, stacking up traffic until twenty or more vehicles were assembled, then sending them onward as a convoy to the next check post twenty or more miles along. At the first such gathering point, Sultan strode forward for a quiet conference with the policeman in charge. Then with the three vehicles in tight formation, and guided by a constable, they pulled onto the rocky shoulder, around the waiting traffic and past the striped pole dropped across the roadway. Quickly accelerating on the other side, with a half smile Sultan commented that the police would allow no one, under any circumstances, to proceed for the next thirty minutes. Whoever sat fuming behind in the long queue of trucks, and whatever their unwholesome motives, they would not see their quarry again this day.

"And who will be the hunter, and who the prey, next time?" wondered Bailey.

For perhaps a mile, Sultan drove silently. "My father was stationed in Bangladesh after partition," he finally said, staring fixedly ahead down the dark road, "when it was still East Pakistan. He told me that was the fascination with hunting tigers."

VOX CLAMANTIS

Cassandra cried, and curs'd th' unhappy hour;
Foretold our fate; but, by the god's decree,
All heard, and none believ'd the prophecy.

—Virgil, "The Aeneid"

FORT BRAGG, NORTH CAROLINA, 1998

Smoke Bomb Hill remained, frozen in time. To either side of the asphalt street, tacky and shimmering in the North Carolina summer, white two-story wooden barracks ranked in identical measured rows, on parade rest since their construction in the 1950s. Resilient clumps of crabgrass and stunted longleaf pines scrabbled tenaciously in the sandy soil.

Now the troops all lived in modern, brick, centrally air-conditioned dormitory housing elsewhere on Fort Bragg. The wooden barracks had evolved into classrooms and unit headquarters, until those too moved into more modern high-rises. Today the old buildings clung to life as offices for obscure small units and staffs, primarily with maintenance and housekeeping roles, without the importance or clout to collocate with the mighty powers on the vast base: the XVIII Airborne Corps, the 82nd Airborne Division, the Special Forces Command and School.

For Lieutenant Colonel Bailey, however, as for generations of Special Forces soldiers before him, "The Hill" would always be alma mater. Here in 1952, in the dawning of the Cold War, a Psychological Warfare Headquarters was formed and quickly spawned the 10th Special Forces Group, dedicated to guerilla warfare, and other esoteric units. Here, in their turn, Bailey and his peers had come, learning at the schoolhouse, earning their green berets, training for Vietnam in the footsteps of legends: "Mad Dog" Shriver, vanished in Cambodia but for rumors on Radio Hanoi; Nick Rowe, one of the very few American prisoners ever to escape from the Viet Cong, gunned down decades later in the streets of Manila by a communist "sparrow team" on a motor scooter; Colonel "Bull" Simon and the Son Te raiders who deliberately crash-landed their helicopter inside a POW camp deep in North Vietnam to fight their way out; and others known only to the secretive, closed society called "Group."

Then as now, surrounding The Hill, insulating it from the outside world, lay the massive, pulsing military engine of Fort Bragg. In a sense unrecognized in Washington or New York, this was the center of world affairs. Not a border skirmish, coup attempt, or even diplomatic fracas erupted anywhere on the planet without the tremors reverberating here at the home of the nation's airborne forces. Staff officers hastily updated contingency plans; logisticians pored over requirements and pre-positioned equipment and supplies; troops rehearsed and prepared to execute on a moment's notice.

The drone of aircraft overhead never ceased, day or night. Fresh-faced paratroopers flew out unceasingly from the Green Ramp on the airbase for training, peacekeeping, and war. Each payday weekend, from up and down the East Coast, hookers arrived at the civilian commuter airport. Disciplined and spit-shined, brawling and profane, this was not part of the East Coast power elite but more the Chicago of Carl Sandburg or the San Francisco of Jack London.

Yet at the center of it all, The Hill of Bailey's memory always would remain a place apart, and Group an order unto themselves. Outside the base, draft dodgers, campus protesters, and attention-seeking celebrities such as Jane Fonda were openly hostile. A hubristic media competed not to report world events but to determine them. Derelict politicians pandered to the winds of public sentiment. Even within the beleaguered Army, Special Forces were considered suspect—elite, reckless, from neither the conventional military mold nor the draftee ranks. Promotions, controlled by centralized boards, came slowly for those who chose to remain apart, and for officers promotion beyond colonel was almost impossible.

Bailey was reminded of Ernest Shackleton's famous, if apocryphal, newspaper advertisement for an expedition to the Antarctic:

"Men Wanted for Hazardous Journey. Small wages, bitter cold, long months of complete darkness, constant danger, safe return doubtful. Honor and recognition in case of success."

Except of course for the honor and recognition part. Beginning with the Gulf War in 1990, all that had begun to change. Tickertape parades, not spitting hippies, greeted the returning troops, and "Thank you for your service" had become as banal as "Have an nice day." He never knew how to respond to either. Somehow it had been easier to snarl back at the world.

Bailey tapped his PIN into the lock of a gate in a chain-link fence that surrounded a plain, windowless building, somewhat larger than its neighbors but of the same era. No sign identified its purpose or inhabitants. Jerking his thoughts away from the past, he stepped through into the future—the first "virtual group." Still specialized, elite, and secretive, the 10th and successor Special Forces groups each now covered specific regions of the globe: Latin America, Europe, Africa, and Asia. Speaking the languages, immersed in the cultures, teams from the groups could be found on average in more than seventy different countries worldwide at any given time, performing missions covert and overt, from combat to humanitarian to military training. But this virtual group had no geographic territory, no teams deployed or otherwise. It literally did not even exist "on paper", but only in electronic messages and databases.

When the time came for boots on the ground, troops would be found, troops with whatever regional experience and skills were required. For the moment just twenty persons constituted the unit, most of them intelligence analysts and operatives. They came from across the Intelligence Community, military and civilian, male and female, and they brought with them their networking skills and their computer links. Only The Old Man, Colonel Owens, and his sergeant major reflected a traditional Special Forces group headquarters.

For the first time since he had received his college degree and draft notice on the same fateful day in 1969, Bailey too was one of the civilians. He had served more than half his career in civilian clothes, but it was still unsettling to formally set his uniform and commission aside. An ironic consequence, he mused, of the emerging thaw between the military establishment and the special operations community. Now that Special Forces officers were progressing to upper levels of command and staff, it was no longer tolerable for a field grade officer to devote his career to hunting a chimera more of the tenth century than the twentieth. Offered no alternative to promotion to full colonel and a posting to the Pentagon, he had, with considerable misgivings, chosen his calling over the uniform. If Group could evolve, so could Bailey.

Inside the building, above a double door that led to a large central bullpen divided into cubicles for the analysts, a white sign read, in block letters: "AMATEURS STUDY TACTICS; PROFESSIONALS STUDY LOGISTICS." —GENERAL OMAR BRADLEY.

The mission of the virtual group was to understand and counter the logistics of terror: the movement of money, trainees, weapons, and operatives around the world, and in particular its chief practitioners, the Saudi Usama bin Laden and his Egyptian deputy, Ayman Zawaheri.

Captain Maclean shivered inside his down sweater, not from the icy cold of the desert false dawn but in anticipation. To all appearances he might have been alone in the barren landscape. To his left and right, invisible in clefts in the rock and under camouflage blankets, his team lay in position. Their Afghan allies and guides, codenamed the Archangel Network during the war against the Soviets, secured a cave and rally point eight hundred meters to the southwest. The two engineers already had crawled forward and secured shape charges under the small bridge that crossed a dry creek bed in the kill zone of the ambush. The silent gray landscape seethed with potential.

On his right a camouflaged form materialized along with his deputy's soft whisper, "We're good. But the guys are going crazy with the waiting. Pull the trigger!"

Captain Maclean sympathized with his team's tension and eagerness for action—on the level of logic. In his gut, though, he felt it differently. It was this sweet, adrenaline-fueled moment, events poised at the tipping point, outcomes unknown, that he lived for. Standing in the dark roaring door of a plane, ready to take the effortless step into freefall. Body rocking in ski boots planted just behind the timer's electric eye, high on a mountainside, as the starter counts down the seconds. (On the circuit they joked about how many languages they could count in fluently, backwards from five to one.) And, of course, this: The Great Game, The Tournament of Shadows, infinitely deadlier and more seductive. Reluctant to see the moment end, but eager as the others to carry out the mission, Maclean hit the "send" button on his silent transmitter. It was time to lure the tiger to the trap.

Across the dry gulch with its explosive-laden bridge, miles up the winding desert track, colorful Bedouin tents sprawled around a small oasis, leather-hooded falcons perched like sentries in their shadowy doorways. Immediately behind, as if sheltering the tiny encampment under its massive wings, lurked the aluminum bulk of a Hercules C-130 air transport, unmarked but for a colorful flag from the Persian Gulf painted on its tail. For fifty weeks each year, this campsite in the middle of the forsaken Afghan southland lay deserted; for ten days or so, it became a center of prestige and power in the Arab world.

For this was a way station on the annual migration across Central Asia of the rarest, and most prized, of game birds: the Houbara Bustard. In pursuit, royal sportsmen flew in from throughout the Persian Gulf with their hunting falcons, for a brief time romantically indulging in the desert austerity of their ancestors before the coming of the petrodollars. As at other exclusive hunting camps around the world, during the long nights deals were struck and arrangements made—financial, political, dynastic.

Afghans were neither Arab nor welcome.

One sole visitor had not flown in, arriving instead overland from Qandahar with his entourage in a convoy of dusty white SUVs. Although exiled from his Saudi homeland, and fearing capture elsewhere, the tall, black-bearded figure in immaculate white robes and gold-threaded headdress was welcomed, even lionized, by the aristocracy of the Persian Gulf in the privacy and anonymity of their remote encampment. Whispered congratulations were exchanged over the dramatic destruction of embassies that represented the decadent West in Nairobi and Dar es Salaam, with the killing of dozens of American diplomats and hundreds of Africans associated with them. Secret plans were laid to fund the next suicide bombing attack on a symbol of the power of The Great Satan—a warship of its proud navy.

In the dimly lit bullpen on Smoke Bomb Hill, Captain Maclean's message that his team was in position scrolled in blocky green letters across twenty computer screens. At one, a figure wearing a Grateful Dead sweatshirt and three day's black beard grunted in satisfaction then with two forefingers fed lines of code into a second terminal. In Abu Dhabi the computer of a large commercial bank blinked to life. From behind several firewalls, in the most restrictive and private of accounts, on coded instructions from al-Qa'ida deputy Zawaheri in Qandahar, Afghanistan, petrodollars intended for the attack on the US Navy instead began to trickle, then cascade, into an account in Karachi controlled by Mullah Omar and the Taliban.

Faithful to its fiducial obligations, the computer in Abu Dhabi promptly alerted, via satellite link to the remote but not entirely primitive hunting camp, both the royal donors and their intended recipient, Usama bin Laden.

The typist leaned back in his chair, interlocked his fingers, and cracked his knuckles. To Bailey, who was watching over his shoulder, he murmured, "There, our virtual goat is staked. Let's see how long it takes to lure our tiger back to Qandahar to sort this out."

Without warning the overhead lights flicked on in the bull-pen, their harsh illumination amplifying Colonel Owens's startling announcement: "ENDEX, people. Rehearsal's over. Shut 'er down. Captain Maclean and his team can go administrative and drive back to the airfield at Fort Huachuca for airlift back. Same for the forward operational base at Fort Hood. The SOCOM CG [Special Operations Command, Commanding General] and I leave Pope Airfield at ten hundred hours for DC. All hands hot-wash [review for lessons learned] as soon as the field elements and I return." The Old Man spun and stalked out of the bullpen, his face flushed and his jaw clenched, veins visibly throbbing just below his bristled white hair. Bailey thought of following him, to check on his health if nothing else, but reconsidered.

"Okay, gentlemen, and ladies, I'm not going to sugarcoat this. They shut us down. We have no op," began Colonel Owens the following morning. "But don't ask me who *they* are. There must have been thirty people packed into the briefing room under the West Wing—more than we've read-in to this whole compartmented program as analysts, staff, and operators since we began. Other than one guy from the J-5 staff at the Pentagon who took us in, I didn't recognize a soul. No cabinet secretaries, no National Security Advisor. Nobody you naively thought was in charge.

"There was one skinny little turd in a suit that must have cost more than my car, literally wringing his hands and whining about 'the integrity of the international banking system.' I'm not making this up. And there was some public relations wonk—corduroy jacket with patches on the elbows, the professorial look, I guess—going on about risking American casualties, and 'the Mogadishu effect,' which he seemed to think happened in the Middle East. When I pointed out that we have the best operators in the world, all volunteers competing like Olympic athletes for opportunities to do high-stakes missions like this, it turned out he wasn't worried about them at all. Just the spectacle of the morning talk shows shoving their mikes in the faces of grieving families.

"I knew it was a done deal when a guy from Justice with a Jersey accent and a pinstripe suit got up and started lecturing about 'contaminated evidence' and 'entrapment.' He was going on about 'discovery' and revealing everything we'd ever done against this target, even this Operational Readiness Exercise, when he tries Usama bin Laden and Ayman Zawaheri in open court in Manhattan. And everyone in the briefing room was nodding their heads, like that's really going to happen. Like any moment now UBL will rob a bank in Chicago, and the FBIs can flash their badges, sleuth out the clues, read him his Miranda rights, convict him before a jury of his peers, and make a TV series about themselves.

" 'Come back when you have a less risky plan,' they said. So there you have it, folks. UBL has lawyered up. You can kill all the night watchmen, gate guards, and drivers you want, but if anyone is identified by name in the intel, you need to capture 'em alive. And you can't trick them, or rob them, or keep anything secret. And no soldiers can risk being killed or captured for the security of the nation. All Silver Stars will be followed by courts martial. Got it? Get back to work!"

Outside the windowless building, its surrounding chain-link fence and cipher-lock gate, a thick morning fog still hid the emerging North Carolina sun and all but the nearest buildings and struggling pines. From every direction, from as far as the ear could hear, out of the fog throbbed a muted tempo: the rhythmic tramp of feet, companies and battalions jogging in time; NCOs setting the pace with cadence calls and traditional "Jody songs"; the formations answering in chorus. Each unit ran invisible and separate, all blending into Fort Bragg's timeless morning rhythm. The ghostly cadence could be from this morning's reveille or from fifty years before.

"Welcome home," murmured Bailey to himself. Approaching in the fog, he imagined he could hear a half-remembered chant:

If I die in a combat zone,
Box me up and ship me home,
Plant me face down in the grass,
So the world can kiss my ass.

GOAT GAME

Riding a horse is not a gentle hobby, to be picked
up and laid down like a game of solitaire.

—Ralph Waldo Emerson

NANGARHAR PROVINCE, AFGHANISTAN, 2001

I t is fast, violent, and played for purses of gold. Teamwork, treachery, and a headless goat. Sometimes described as playing rugby while mounted on fighting stallions and using a dead body for the ball, *buzkashi* (goat game) was introduced into Afghanistan in the fourteenth century by Mogul invaders from the steppes of Central Asia. The game sunk deep and enduring roots in the flinty soil of Afghan national character.

The first game lasted about twenty minutes, after which the players took a water break, and Bailey mounted a borrowed horse with the eager, amused help of a dozen bystanders. One man pointed to Bailey's glasses and indicated he would be glad to hold them. Bailey turned his head to show that they were secured with a neoprene retaining band and would be okay, but the bystander looked doubtful. Under the deep, blocky saddle, upholstered not with leather but with red-patterned, woven-wool carpeting, the wiry little gray neckreined and responded to Bailey's seat like a good cow pony. One of the dismounted organizers picked up the heavy black "buz" by a stiff protruding leg and offered it to the American, pantomiming a photo op. Pride forbade accepting such a privilege for the *ferangi*, of course. In Afghanistan one must get his goat the hard way.

The "umpire" dropped the headless carcass in a circle sketched in the rocky field in front of the spectators, like a hockey referee dropping the puck, then jumped rapidly backward as a dozen horses and riders surged forward. A rising cloud of dust from almost fifty straining, shuffling hooves partially obscured the scene.

With a high-pitched cry, one rider reared his horse, plunging forward to the center with steel-shod front hooves flailing at eye level. As his horse came down astride the carcass, the rider ducked his torso and right arm down to snatch it from the ground, left hand clutching the pommel of his saddle and left leg curled upward to counterbalance. While he was in this vulnerable position, face inches from the milling hooves, his teammates forged in beside him like a wedge of bodyguards. Opposing players sought to break his grip, charging into his horse with their own, whipping horse and rider indiscriminately with the thumb-thick braided leather quirts that were the only weapons allowed on the field.

Play had resumed.

Several young riders greeted Bailey with shy, welcoming smiles as he trotted his horse carefully at the edge of the milling crowd of horsemen. One portly older gent, arrayed in a threadbare tweed sport coat and a natty white turban, turned his horse aside and courteously motioned him toward the raucous cloud of dust in the center. Bailey declined, instead making a great show of getting used to his unfamiliar mount. In fact he wanted no more of that melee than did the many other riders out at the fringe.

Nearest to, and farthest from, the goat, two types of power players were easily identified. Atop the flat roof of a mud-walled building that flanked the field, Hajji Ali sat above the fray, surrounded by two dozen honored guests. Upon a sea of dark-red carpets, their ample girths supported by sturdy wooden chairs somehow wrestled up the rickety ladder that provided the only access, he and the local aristocracy drank tea and exchanged knowledgeable commentary on the qualities of notable horses and riders. Upon each score, Hajji Ali bestowed lavish prize money on the winning rider and his teammates, with a confident, easy banter that engulfed riders and spectators in raucous laughter.

This was the first tournament since the Taliban had outlawed all forms of play, from the national sport of buzkashi to the flying of kites by children. Every symbol proclaimed the obvious, that Hajji Ali, tribal chieftain and warlord, once again ruled this roost: he put up the prize money, rewarded the winners, enforced the peace among fractious clans during the period of the buzkashi tournament, lavished gifts and feasts upon the notables for miles around. It was an expensive but essential display of power in a land where power ebbed and flowed like the surging tide of horses on the field of play.

Under the appreciative eyes of the rooftop aristocracy, the center of the dusty melee and the carcass of the goat itself were ruled by the *chapandaz:* elite, professional horsemen mounted and girt to play and win this violent contest. The headless carcass must travel from the winner's circle, changing hands through many violent encounters at full gallop, around a pole at the far end of the field of play, and thence back to be dropped exactly where it started. And winner take all; only the successful rider at the end and his teammates would be rewarded with Hajji Ali's fluttering rupees, regardless of the heroic feats of horsemanship en route.

Two teams of four could be distinguished by their uniform dress, although in Afghan fashion there seemed to be no standard to define what constituted a uniform. One group of traditionalists wore green tunics belted at the waist with wide white sashes, and baggy pants wrapped tightly below the knee with strips of cloth resembling World War I puttees. Skullcaps rimmed with bands of dusky fur accented their narrow-eyed and flat-nosed Mongol faces. The modernist quartet sported black leather jackboots, padded fatigue jackets, and ribbed Soviet tankers' helmets. Bailey chose not to dwell on how they had obtained this raiment.

Between these poles of power, the tribal warlord sponsors and the professional athletes of the most violent game on Earth, ranged the entire spectrum of Afghan society. In Afghanistan's unique compound of tribal hierarchy and libertarianism, distinctions between spectator and participant are murky, not least in buzkashi, where the field of play is anywhere the hoard chooses to gallop, frequently forcing spectators to sprint for their lives.

From distant windows that overlooked the field of play, and from benches on the surrounding hillsides, flashes of color hinted at women and girls observing from afar. Surrounding the field stood groups of men and boys, the graybeards behind stone walls or atop steep knolls. The younger and bolder crept forward, ever closer to better vantage points, until inevitably the galloping scrum of horses surged their way and those on foot fled like the runners at Pamplona.

Closer still were the equestrian gentry, every man and boy who owned or could borrow a horse. On the fringe of play, they surrounded the chapandaz fighting for possession of the buz, and followed the mad gallops around the goalposts. On occasion the bolder made brief passes at capturing the goat, but for the most part they were content to posture in front of their pedestrian fellows and to enjoy their privileged view of the real action.

Had he come here thirty, or even twenty, years before, Bailey knew that neither the twenty-year-old athlete nor the thirty-year-old soldier would have been satisfied anywhere but in the center of the scrum. Now, however, he was content to count himself among these outer ranks. All, on this special day, were part of the buzkashi.

Not long after, in a remote mountain village not far away, an American Special Forces team arrived at the marketplace in hot pursuit of al-Qa'ida and their Taliban allies. From the backs of three banged-up Toyota Hilux pickup trucks spilled a dozen Afghans, readily identifiable as American allies by their shiny new AK-47s and rocket-propelled grenade launchers, and by the highly prized military-issue, cold-weather clothing items they wore. Several were arrayed in bulky brown polyester-fleece jackets and matching trousers with button flaps on the back, designed for the US Army as undergarments for arctic conditions, which made the soldiers resemble sinister, heavily armed teddy bears.

The six Americans, in dark fleece jackets and caps adorned with Mountain Hardware, North Face, and Marmot logos, cargo pants, and GORE-TEX boots, could have blended in on the streets of Vail or Steamboat Springs, were it not for their long unkempt hair and beards, and the stubby, black, businesslike M4 assault rifles slung across their chests. It was December 2001, a short time but a long trail from Manhattan.

Directly above, in an impossibly blue, cloudless winter sky, a dark speck traced a brilliant white, perfectly circular contrail. Without a single glance upward, every man and boy in the valley was aware of the looming presence of the B-52, its load of magically guided destruction, and the ability of the Americans to call down the wrath of *Wash-ing-ton* with a whisper into the microphones clipped to their shoulders. Colonel Bailey remembered similar forays two decades earlier, his safety then ensured in more traditional fashion by Mujahedin pickets on every high knoll on the ridgelines to either side of his route. Then, as now, although the throngs of curious tribesmen were overtly friendly, he was mindful of the Pushtun saying "Unarmed, you are my enemy" and was grateful for the overwatch.

"Intrepid Afghan warriors, my ass!" exclaimed Captain Maclean. "How these guys whipped the Soviets or the Brits or anyone else I'll never know." Flecks of premature gray tinged the beard that covered his hollow cheeks and the otherwise dark hair that escaped beneath his wool afghan hat, and his hard black eyes reflected more than one campaign.

"Hajji Ali, supposedly the great warlord, sits on his butt in his palace down in the valley, sucking down tea and money and guns. Claims he can raise a thousand warriors. Well, there might be a thousand sons of bitches running around the hills, but when it comes right down to it, there's not more than two, maybe three dozen real warriors.

"Now, there are exceptions. Some absolute crazies. Naimullah—when we got to the end of the road for the pickups, he and his six men went up that mountain like goats in shower shoes. Found that bunch of Arabs and East Africans in the cave at Rocky Point and called back the targeting data on his walkie-talkie. When we told them to get out of there, they stayed instead, calling back reports from the middle of the damndest B-52 strike I've ever seen. The whole damn mountain was rockin' and rollin', and there's Naimullah praising Allah for every hit! Couldn't see him for the smoke and barely heard him on the radio between the five-hundred pounders coming in.

"And Muhammad With-No-Other-Names: a scrawny little dude, maybe a hundred and twenty pounds if his *shalwar kameez* was soaking wet. Black beard like a *mullah*, little white skullcap on his head. Maybe ten men in his squad, and two trucks so beat up you couldn't tell what color they were supposed to be. I didn't think anything of them until I suddenly realized those two trucks were idling along as smooth as anything on a new car lot in the

States. So I looked again, and every one of those ten men carried an AK-47 as clean as if it had just come from the factory. Even the rounds in the magazines had been emptied out and wiped free of the grit that's everywhere in Afghanistan. Plus the usual rocket-propelled grenades and other accoutrements, all in the same condition. I asked Muhammad With-No-Other-Names what they were all about, and he told me they were there for the twenty-million-dollar reward for Usama bin Ladin, nothing more, nothing less. They vanished up the Tir Garagh valley into the mountains that first morning, and I haven't seen them since. Maybe they're still on the hunt...hope so!"

Captain Maclean paused, shifted his slung carbine to a more comfortable position, and glanced at his "special advisor." Sometimes he felt uncomfortable having a retired colonel around, but more often he was grateful for the sounding board and the sometimes-Delphic voice of experience.

"But those are the exceptions," he emphasized. "Most of these jerks are running up and down the mountain in our trucks, carrying our guns, trying to impress each other, not doing jack!" he sputtered to an exasperated halt. "And try to get Hajji Ali up here to lead from the front? Organize these assholes into even a battalion-size force to assault the caves or place blocking forces along the border? It'll snow in Saigon before he puts down his teacup."

"Have you ever played buzkashi?" asked Colonel Bailey quietly.

RINGING IN THE NEW

Forward, forward let us range,
Let the great world spin for ever
Down the ringing grooves of change.

—Alfred, Lord Tennyson, "Locksley Hall"

AFGHANISTAN, 2001–2002

Like strange creatures adrift in a nighttime sea, longneck bottles of Corona glowed phosphorescent green and meandered, waist high, about the darkened hall. Early into the manic evening, it had been discovered that miniature chemical light sticks—emergency recognition signals from survival kits—slid neatly into the open beer bottles, and now the volunteer bartenders slipped them unbidden into each departing bottle. A single strand of colored Christmas lights, strung along the walls above the windows, provided the only other illumination.

Behind a knot of people surrounding the ambassador, the Afghan hotel staff in stiff white shirts and frayed black suit jackets poured glass after glass of Champagne, arranged the sparkling flutes in intricate rows on a table, and when the Americans failed to abandon their Coronas, drank the Champagne themselves. Reinforcements arrived in waves from the kitchen. It was the final day of 2001 and the end of a six-year drought in Kabul.

At midnight the blond-bearded embassy doctor, cargo pants topped by a red-and-yellow floral-print Polynesian shirt from some other deployment, climbed upon a chair, swayed once before catching his balance, and called the room to silence with a battery-powered megaphone. The Afghan staff circulated unsteadily, handing out sheets bearing the words to "Auld Lang Syne." After leading a rousing rendition of verses one and two, in the middle of the third, Doc's voice slowed, the microphone dropped to his side, and, with a roll of his eyes toward the ceiling, like the crystal ball at Times Square the doctor descended limply from on high into the waiting arms of the crowd below. He would not emerge from his little dispensary down the hall until late the following day, hungover but unrepentant.

It was just six the following morning, however, when Abdullah pulled a boxy green Land Rover Defender up to the front portico of the hotel, where Colonel Bailey met him and loaded in his duffel. Bailey had been unable to find anyone in the kitchen, and he felt a surge of gratitude when the old interpreter reached behind the front seat to produce a thermos of hot, milky tea, and flatbread still warm from the market.

A throwback to the days before the coming of the communists and the warlords and the Taliban fanatics, Abdullah had learned his English, and his loyalty, in a motor pool for the US Agency for International Development, where he maintained a fleet of white Land Rovers in the days of the king, when last the Americans and European nations had come to help build his country. Abdullah claimed—and Bailey was never quite sure whether to take him at face value or to take it as some kind of wry Afghan humor—to have introduced the concept of the speed bump to Afghanistan, in revolt against constant dents and crunches to his beloved Land Rovers. Given the profusion of spine-jarring barriers that randomly obstructed every Afghan road, punctuating every bazaar, village, and check post, Bailey wasn't sure why one would brag about such an innovation, but the old man loved to repeat the tale, and Bailey loved him for it.

Abdullah eased his vehicle into gear and out onto the nearly deserted streets of Kabul. Passing on their left the former soccer stadium, used until recently by the Taliban for public executions, they left the dreadful old year behind and drove south into a new, pink dawn.

Beginning high above their heads, ending far behind and below, a serpentine convoy of pickups and cargo trucks wound its way up an enormous rocky ravine, each hairpin switchback slowing the vehicles to a crawl, the larger ones loudly grinding gears and engulfing their cargos of soldiers in black diesel smoke. Now in mid-winter there was not a scrap of vegetation to be seen on the vast slopes of broken rock to either side, and the riverbed below was a dry jumble of stones. Colonel Bailey had not seen a human other than their own party since they began the steep climb, but perched on occasional distant rock buttresses were huge, adobe-walled fortresses, each a silent village unto itself.

A crude roadblock, a single long pole set on a tripod with a rock lashed to its butt end as counterbalance, marked where the road topped the ridge and began its long, sinuous descent into the great bowl of Gardez Province. Beside the road a single-story stone building, two low-ceilinged rooms beneath a flat mud roof, offered the only meager comforts for the checkpoint garrison. No lofty mountain peaks glistened above; no green agricultural terraces or wooded valleys beckoned from below. Desolate, broken rock lay above and below, ahead and behind.

The convoy, an American Special Forces detachment and two companies of their Afghan allies, halted at the crest for stragglers to catch up, while a reconnaissance team checked the road ahead. From this point forward lay the unknown, for no American had traveled this route since at least the Soviet invasion thirty years before, and even their Afghan allies were from the north, without tribal links or kinship here. The Taliban had been routed as a coherent military force, but the powerful Pushtun clans of this region were as yet untested.

Years ago Colonel Bailey had heard firsthand reports from Mujahedin commanders about fearsome ambushes of Soviet columns along the road they had just ascended, and he had later read accounts by the Soviet soldiers who had nicknamed it The Road of Death. He had studied satellite imagery of the provincial capital ahead in minute detail, searching for ways his guerilla allies might capture it, after the forces from Kabul abandoned the treacherous road completely and supplied the town and its garrison entirely by air. He and a small number of companions had chafed under headquarters restrictions limiting the American officers to the other side of the border. To come now in person, to drive the routes and meet the inhabitants of this formerly forbidden battlefield, as the spearhead of a new, victorious force, was unique in Colonel Bailey's career. It was a source of considerable satisfaction and pride, and a sweet irony five years after his "retirement from active duty."

The mountain road emerged onto rocky plains, and the convoy halted where a precariously listing antenna tower and a two-story building—walls cracked and discolored, windows broken out, and all electric wiring and plumbing long since looted—identified an abandoned Soviet-era radio station. Behind stretched acres of brush and eroded rocky badlands, a graveyard of rusted hulks of tanks and trucks mounted with rocket launchers. Incongruously, two teenage boys soon showed up to fire up one ancient battle tank and proudly demonstrate slow, clanking circles to the astonished strangers.

As the boys finished their armored perambulation, the visitors realized that the shaking ground was more than the passing of the lumbering war machine, the deep rumble more than the Harley roar of its diesel engine. The antenna tower swayed like a fly rod, and adobe chunks spalled off the walls of the radio station, bursting into clouds of dust where they hit the rocky ground. The small earthquake tore at the decrepit building as if the mountains themselves were determined to obliterate all trace of the Soviet invaders.

Over the flat hood of the Land Rover, Bailey saw the dark silhouette of an ancient fortress that loomed above the town, a huge round tower atop a rocky hill, crenulated sheer stone walls, the long barrel of an antiaircraft machine gun visible atop one turret, a green pennant flying from the summit. It squatted like a piece of the rocky landscape, as impervious to the seismic tremors as to the wind and rain.

From seats of honor along the end wall of a large council chamber within the fortress, the four Americans regarded the gathered assembly; sixty or seventy men in total jammed the room, Bailey estimated. Twenty-five of them, the shura council members, sat in chairs in a rough square that included the visitors, and as each arrived he seemed to know exactly where he was to sit. A throng of men packed the space behind, and boys peered in through open windows. All were dressed, armed, bearded, and turbaned in astonishing variety. Bailey and his companions had passed more than the mountain barrier this morning; they were no longer in the dour north, where men wore drab long-tailed shirts, dark vests, and the ubiquitous rolled wool pakool hats.

Eldest and oddest of all was a patriarch with a long, wispy white beard, lean, sunken cheeks, one eye the milky white of advanced cataracts, and a voluminous white turban accented with a tall gold-colored brush. Around his narrow waist was wrapped a yellow sash, or cummerbund, supporting on his left hip a curved cavalry saber almost as long as its bearer was tall. Upon his arrival the men seated nearby politely leapt to seize his elbows and gently maneuver him and his sword into a chair.

Along the side wall to Bailey's right sat a figure in white cotton shirt and trousers and tailored black vest, with a neatly trimmed black beard and white skullcap, writing in a small, leather-bound notebook with a gold ballpoint pen. He had sought out the Americans before the meeting, introducing himself in English as a doctor. Bailey was not surprised by the presence of Pakistani Intelligence, but he found the boldness of it remarkable— the man was practically in uniform—and he wondered whom this "doctor" had dealt with, and on what business, before this day. Within the neat rectangle of exotic dress and elaborate welcoming speeches would be many old Mujahedin fighters, a few Taliban fanatics, local warlords immersed in tribal politics and feuds, opium and timber smugglers, tribal elders from all the region's villages and valleys, merchants from the town, and influential clerics. Tomorrow's enemies and tomorrow's friends, but only Allah knew which were which.

As the formal round of greeting speeches worked its way around the square of elders, Bailey recalled exotic black-and-white photos of the legendary nineteenth-century British political officers and adventurers who first had planted the stamp of the British Raj in the Punjab and the North-West Frontier: John Nicholson, Henry Lawrence, Major William Hodson of Hodson's Horse, in meetings exactly like this. And, a generation or so later, his own particular hero and namesake, Colonel F.M. Bailey, exploring forbidden Tibet, living underground and hunted by the communists in Tashkent during the First World War, later playing the Great Game across the breadth of Central Asia. Bailey had been raised as a boy on these romantic histories, but even then he knew them to be part of a bygone era, far removed from modern reality. Yet here he sat, as if the twentieth century had never existed. And, he reminded himself wryly, of those names he had just ticked off, only F.M. Bailey had died of natural causes.

Atop the flat dirt roof of the guard shack at the top of the pass, Colonel Bailey, Captain Maclean, and Abdullah sat under the stars, sunk to their chins in sleeping bags to stave off the mountain cold. The two suffocating rooms below were crowded shoulder to shoulder with an indistinguishable mob of Afghans and Americans, all sitting or lying on the floor in a vain attempt to avoid the suffocating black wood smoke that poured from two cherry-red stoves vented only by stovepipes stuck out of small windows. Tiny campfires winked up and down the surrounding rocky hillsides, where the Afghan troops huddled beneath blankets and kept watch down the southern road.

"This is like the mother of all hangovers," Captain Maclean commented. "We begin the day exchanging toasts with the ambassador and patting ourselves on the backs for routing the Taliban out of Kabul. We end it making a dry bivouac after dark, run out of that Podunk province by a hoard of frenzied Pushtuns."

"Don't forget time travel back to the nineteenth century. And the earthquake at the Soviet radio station. Write this one in your diary. This is a New Year's Day you'll remember for the rest of your life," Bailey added, perhaps advice to the younger captain, perhaps a reminder to himself.

"The year is young, and already we're off to an interesting beginning," he continued. "Respect and honor. Honor and respect. *Izaat* and *nang*. *Nang* and *izaat*. Always good starting points. We know they respect our B-52s, and the elders still honor us for standing by them against the Soviets. One of them today even remembered me from the camps, told me 'Thank you,' and called me *jihadi* as he hugged me before the council meeting. Now we must show respect for their land and honor their tribes by waiting outside their border for an invitation and an alliance.

"I thought making camp outside the town, at the radio station, would be sufficient. One of the elders even suggested it. As we learned from the overhead surveillance report we got this evening, though, that wasn't enough for some of the troublemakers, the several hundred young hotheads who were gathering to confront us. Easy enough to defend ourselves, of course, but that would have meant either a firefight between the locals and our troops from tribes in another province, or an American airstrike on teenagers who think they're defending their tribal honor. No way to start the New Year. Better to sit back, play by their rules, and let the elders in the shura council work it out."

Abdullah nodded in agreement, the long curls of his white beard rasping on his nylon sleeping bag. "In the north, in ancient Balkh where the Turkmen breed the best buzkashi horses in all Afghanistan," he said, "in what you call the ninth century after Christ, our great poet Rabi'a wrote, *'I knew not when I rode the high-blood steed, the more that I pulled, the less he would heed.'* On any proud horse, if you pull on his rein or push your leg on his flank, he will pull or push against you in resistance. But if he respects you as a rider and you just lift your leg slightly from his flank, he will flow in that direction, looking for you. This is a time to ride lightly but surely, Sa'bs."

THE FREEDOM OF THE PRESS

Freedom's just another word
for nothin' left to lose.

—Kris Kristofferson, "Me and Bobby McGee"

AFGHANISTAN, 2002

At barely walking speed, Bailey eased his darkened van through one last rocky ditch and up onto the relatively smooth, hard-packed apron at the end of a desolate and unpaved airstrip. No moon had yet risen, but overhead an impossibly bright Milky Way cast a pale glow over the barren landscape. Behind, he heard the raspy, irregular gasps of the wounded reporter and the heavy breathing of the team medic, Josh, as he struggled in the lurching vehicle to keep pressure on her blood-soaked thigh and IV fluids flowing into her arm to stave off encroaching shock, and death. The vehicle was heavy with the smells of blood and fear, in addition to the usual Afghan odors of dust and wet wool.

Every instinct urged to hurry onward; to get this over; to deliver the unwelcome, dying passenger to the waiting Air Force hospital C-130 that had reportedly made an emergency landing for their patient somewhere on this long abandoned runway. But three years of volunteering his Saturday nights, for the emergency medical practice (or maybe for the excitement), with an ambulance company in one of the grittier suburbs of Detroit had taught Bailey to race like hell to the scene, when the situation is still unknown and the victim has no help. Then, with the patient aboard, time slows down, and the driver must give the patient and attending medic as smooth a ride as possible, while both play their indispensable roles to hang on to life.

Even more years, and more practice, had taught Colonel Bailey that racing up upon any Afghan guard post, enemy or friendly, in the dark could result only in a hail of automatic weapons fire. He wasn't absolutely sure who controlled this southern end of the airstrip, but he was certain he wanted to live long enough to find out. The van never exceeded second gear.

From the darkness ahead, a figure appeared, blanket shrouded in the cold night air but with the outline of its AK-47 unmistakable. Bailey stopped the vehicle quickly, straining not to jolt the passengers behind. Without being told, Abdullah eased out of the passenger seat and hurried forward, unarmed, to confront the shadowy sentry. Not for the first time, Bailey watched the old interpreter with admiration. He appeared to be sixty or more years of age, with a long white beard falling in ringlets across his chest, and a single crooked tooth visible beneath a yellowed mustache. Afghanistan aged men quickly.

Abdullah's courage, though, and his air of confidence as he strode into the dark unknown on behalf of his American allies, armed only with his long white beard, were indomitable. Ahead in the darkness, the two shrouded figures converged briefly then separated, and Abdullah reappeared in the passenger seat. "It is well, Sa'b," said the old man quietly. "In front another fifty meters will be a soldier from the airplane. This Afghan guard says to approach him very calmly—he is frightened."

They were not to advance immediately, however. The C-130 had sunk a set of wheels in soft sand while attempting to turn, and the pilot was trying desperately to extract his vulnerable aircraft. Bailey leaned back in the driver's seat, closed his eyes, and tried to imagine what could go wrong next.

The long and dangerous day had begun mid-morning at the provincial governor's compound, with the arrival of two hired cars full of reporters from Kabul. One young man, hung with SLR cameras mounted with long white telephoto lenses and black lens hoods, accosted Bailey as he navigated the pungent crowd of supplicants in the governor's antechamber and acted offended when Bailey wordlessly brushed him off. From long experience Bailey shared most of his peers' contempt for journalists, voyeurs in the making of world events. He had thought little of the encounter until late afternoon, when the commander of their Afghan forces had come to the radio room and operations center, explaining that a group of crazy journalists had arrived at one of the base perimeter sentry points, demanding entry. They were angry and scared, almost in a panic, and unwilling to take the inevitable "no" for an answer.

When Bailey arrived at the guard post, through a cacophony of shouted demands and interjections he gradually was able to piece together the story of a disastrous afternoon. Evidently not content with their risky but uneventful foray from Kabul to the front lines, and ignoring the fact that the special operations base and the governor's compound were located where they were for sound reasons, the journalists persuaded their hired drivers and translators to take them fifteen miles farther down the road, to a town Bailey knew to be still solidly within the Taliban sphere.

At first it seemed that fortune did favor the bold, or the naive. In the bustling, dusty marketplace, they were able to take pictures and conducted interviews with shopkeepers about their "peaceful" crossroads bazaar. It was unremarkable material but for the distant and dangerous location; the journalists knew they had valuable currency for their editors and for the underground journalists' bar in a private room of the Hotel Continental in Kabul.

Soon, though, their translators grew nervous, pointing out increasing numbers of long-bearded young men hanging out in the bazaar, black eyes boldly staring at the visitors with neither smile nor greeting. Discomforted, the reporters broke off their interviews, snapped a few last photos, and piled into their hired vans for a precipitous return journey. Ten miles up the road, as their hired vans slowed through a congested village, crawling at walking pace over the speed bump that defined the marketplace, they never saw the hard-eyed young man who had earlier shadowed them through their photo ops and interviews, nor the hand grenade he dropped through a carelessly open back window.

They knew only the surprisingly muted thump that tore through the vehicle, and the shocking volume of blood that welled from their colleague's shredded thigh, dripping loudly onto the vehicle's bare metal floor. In an instant, they were no longer spectators. There was no public's right to know; there was no First Amendment and no privileged class sheltered behind it, demanding access to the most confidential of government activities and the most private of individuals' tragedies and joys. There was only a frantic search for bandages that failed to stop the inexorable pulse of blood, and a desperate race north in hope of aid and sanctuary.

Aid they found at the perimeter of the special operations base, where the commander did agree, reluctantly and profanely, to take responsibility for the grievously wounded reporter. They found no sanctuary, though; the commander brusquely told the clamoring but uninjured remainder to get the hell out of his battle space and go back to Kabul the way they had come. "Tell 'em to call Charles Ali for a ride in the f***ing CBN Network ambulance," the grizzled operative muttered as he stalked back into his mud-walled compound.

In the tightly knit special operations community, probably every American on the base had heard some version of the treacherous event the commander was referring to. Colonel Bailey suspected he was the only one, however, who knew that the impassioned speaker actually had been on that other dusty street, in a different decade and a different continent, and Bailey appreciated his bitter irony in its awful detail.

A deck of low, gray, winter monsoon clouds welled up from the Indian Ocean and hung over the semi-desert landscape, but as yet no rain had reached the dusty African earth. Pastel shreds of plastic bags swirled in little dust devils between decrepit mud and brick, single-story shops and barren rocky fields. The highway stretched northeast, ultimately to reach the distant capital, barren and devoid of traffic, while fifty feet to one side, behind intermittent repair shops and makeshift food stalls, a rutted track guided a stream of dusty, battered trucks parallel to the deserted highway. Years of civil war had left the highway an un-navigable mine-field, the main route between cities now this parallel, rutted track cross country.

Even there, however, vehicles were not immune to the scourge of land-mines. The four Americans' hearts sank as they pulled their Land Cruiser slowly forward through a milling crowd and saw their comrades' green Nissan Patrol perched precariously on its roof, the left front wheel and fender entirely gone, oil and fuel dripping from a crushed engine block to soak immediately into the dry African earth. The prone body of the driver sprawled lifeless a dozen feet away, only the torn and stained desert fatigues identifying it as their former teammate.

For the moment the body lay unattended, and the shock and sense of outrage that a humanitarian mission could in a moment turn so horri-bly wrong was put on hold. Two Americans from the destroyed SUV, one unscathed and the other oblivious to a blood-soaked sleeve, applied a tour-niquet to the mangled leg of a third, assisted by civilians from a nearby International Red Cross medical clinic. Two of the new arrivals hastily jumped in to move the rapidly growing throng of onlookers back from the scene, for their own safety from additional land mines as well as to guard *against further violence. A third rapidly assembled the spider web of a satellite radio antenna on the hood of their Land Cruiser, aligned it carefully toward a point in the cloud-draped sky, and called out urgently for a Marine Corps medevac helicopter.*

Glancing up from their urgent tasks in response to shouts from the gawking crowd, the Americans were alarmed to see a white Land Rover push deliberately past the makeshift barriers that now blocked access fifty meters from the explosion site. Rolling forward directly toward the overturned Patrol, it stopped only when shouted commands were reinforced by raised automatic carbines. Before any explanation for this defiant intrusion could be demanded, it became unnecessary. From a rear door emerged a video cameraman, the universally recognized three-letter logo of his network emblazoned on the side of his camera. He was immediately joined from the shotgun seat by the equally recognizable icon of modern combat journalism. With his flashing black eyes and hair, dark aquiline features, and slight Middle Eastern accent hinting of secret knowledge unavailable to American provincials, Charles Ali was the current media darling of the war zones, successor to the "Skud Stud" of Gulf War fame.

Imperiously demanding to know what was going on, the identities and mission of the team members, and the name and unit of the casualty, Charles Ali protested when his cameraman was prevented from filming the lifeless body. He needed information immediately, he announced, because he was overdue in the capitol to provide a satellite-feed report to his network. His retreat with his crew and driver to the perimeter boundary seemed more motivated by that impending deadline than by the demands of the rescue team.

Heavy cloud cover and impending rains added to the difficulty and danger of an already uncertain medevac. As they waited for a response from flight operations, the Americans contemplated the only alternative, evacuating their two wounded comrades overland, two hundred or more miles down the already deadly, rutted track through the scrubland, in the white local van hired and equipped by the International Red Cross as a rudimentary ambulance.

That option was to last only moments, however. Checking again at the perimeter, the team saw the CBN vehicle and cameraman still filming from a distance, trying to glean whatever could be exploited of the tragedy. The Red Cross makeshift ambulance, however, pulled out as they watched in helpless frustration, and drove off toward the capitol, Charles Ali in the passenger seat on his way to make his video report, and the local driver three fifty-dollar bills richer.

Luckily, twenty minutes later a Blackhawk helicopter chattered out of the overhead cloudbank to make a seamless extraction of the casualties. Their companions remaining on the ground, however, were members of a small tribe, with a very long memory.

To no one's surprise, least of all Bailey's, the base commander's reluctance to take responsibility for the wounded civilian soon proved justified. The base's facilities were rudimentary, and while the Special Forces medics were among the best in the world at coping with battlefield trauma, they quickly determined that without major surgery they could keep the reporter alive no more than hours. What had begun by granting access to the base and to field treatment escalated almost immediately to requests for any available medevac aircraft, with not just the huge expenses but also the risks to aircrews flying a nighttime mission through Afghanistan's rugged mountains to the vague front lines.

Every man on the base was aware that these aircrews, whom they seldom knew as other than disembodied voices on the radio, would without hesitation risk their lives to evacuate any American soldier who went down in this vicious war. And every man deeply resented the idea that their guardians were to be placed at risk on behalf of a civilian who had no business being there, who in the past could very well have betrayed their security for the sake of a headline, or who might do so in the future if they succeeded in saving her life.

Military decisions are not based on resentments, however, and the struggle to save a life continued, as all knew it must. As the hours passed, the medics reported that the woman's vital systems were only partly stabilized; it was now doubtful that she could survive an unpressurized helicopter evacuation over the mountain ranges between the base and Kabul. Then, at the literal eleventh hour, one hour before midnight, a miracle presented itself. A hospital evacuation plane, a specially equipped Hercules C-130 with a surgical team aboard, was in the air nearby and would divert to a long-abandoned Soviet airfield near the base.

Lined up inside the narrow archway exiting the two-story adobe walls of their big, rectangular compound, a base Land Cruiser and the hired Toyota HiAce van from Kabul that Bailey had appropriated that afternoon to bring in the wounded reporter were followed by three pickup trucks full of Afghan guards bristling with rocket-propelled grenades and Kalashnikovs. *More like an Afghan funeral procession than a medical rescue*, thought Colonel Bailey wryly. From the looks of the small, blanket-shrouded form that they had transferred from the medical tent back into the van, it might yet be either.

Much later, Bailey hunched his shoulders and stood behind the van until the scouring blast of air and sand from the C-130's four massive propellers washed past and the painful high whine of the engines receded to a dull drone then faded entirely into the night sky. Their charge was turned over, her still form visible on an operating table even before the hydraulic ramp at the back of the huge plane silently rose and blocked his view.

"It is a good thing," murmured Abdullah, breaking the sudden silence from the darkness beside Bailey. "A stranger who seeks succor at your hearth must be aided and defended. Even to the death. Even if they are from an enemy tribe. That is *pukhtunwali,* the code of the Pushtuns. Your honor and that of your tribe are undiminished. Allah is merciful."

Bailey thought he could detect a slight smile on the face of the old man, and a glint of starlight on his single tooth.

WHEN PUSHTUN COMES TO SHOVE

Noble kings and princes
Would bow whene'er they came,
Pirate ships would lower their flag
When Puff roared out his name.

—Peter, Paul and Mary, "Puff, the Magic Dragon"

AFGHANISTAN, 2002

From deep within his sleeping bag, Colonel Bailey woke to the sound of the cook's hatchet splitting kindling, and the bleating of a goat. Gratefully he slipped deeper into the down cocoon, anticipating the bright day ahead but willing the sun to top the eastern ridges before he needed to emerge. It was the first day of Eid al-Adha, the Big Eid, the most joyous holiday of the Islamic calendar.

In the afternoon, after families returned from the mosque, Bailey, with Abdullah to translate, along with the chief of the local shura council, would drive out and distribute candy in a dozen surrounding villages. The children, little girls and boys alike, would all be dressed in their holiday finest, fingernails painted gaudy colors, palms sticky from sweets. The boys would mob the cars as soon as they spied them entering the village, while fathers supervised watchfully from the side of the road, holding their little girls' hands and seeing that they got a share of the loot, and mothers watched from shadowed doorways and windows. The customs of Big Eid and Easter were remarkably similar, and for two months Bailey had been hoarding treats in anticipation from care packages forwarded by school children, civic organizations, and church groups in the States.

The goat made all the difference.

When he had gone to bed the night before, Bailey had doubted that his Eid celebration would be possible, and despite a deep exhaustion he had lain awake, mentally replaying the last several tense, contentious days. Initially welcoming the arrival of the team of Americans into his tribal area, professing friendship and protection by his tribal warriors, Hajji Abdul Khan Zadran recently had become petulant and demanding. His formerly daily visits to the base for endless cups of tea had grown infrequent, and when he did show up it was to demand money and weapons.

A certain amount of that was to be expected of course. The primary bone of contention, unspoken by either party, was the Americans' insistence upon providing salaries and weapons directly to the tribesmen whom Hajji Abdul sent to guard the base–rather than routing everything through the old warlord himself. This reduced the opportunities for large amounts to disappear directly into Hajji Abdul's coffers, although he and subordinate leaders undoubtedly still demanded kickbacks from the men they assigned this lucrative duty. Trickle-down extortion aside, however, the practice also struck a blow to the traditional tribal leadership structure, symbolically and financially bonding the men and their loyalty to the strangers.

From their first arrival in the valley—from their first arrival in Afghanistan actually—the famously independent-minded Americans and equally libertarian Afghans took one another's measure across a cultural gulf of centuries. Both were fascinated by this new relationship, sometimes amusing, sometimes contentious, always heavily armed on both sides. The stakes were high, worthy of warriors: honor, pride, great revenge and great wealth.

Some of the rules had never been taught in Special Forces training at Fort Bragg. Two weeks ago Colonel Bailey had stood, exasperated, in the dusty market square, surrounded by a milling, shouting crowd of perhaps fifty Afghans. Staff Sergeant Rabin, the team heavy-weapons NCO, stood nervously at one corner of the square, behind the crowd and back to a wall, carbine unobtrusive but ready, fiddling with the switch of his radio, regretting having volunteered to get off the base by escorting their advisor into town. Four extravagantly painted cargo trucks idled in a row along the street, pumping clouds of oily diesel smoke into the air as their Pakistani drivers formed a noisy huddle, waving fists full of paperwork in Bailey's face.

Raggedly dressed men and boys from the crowd swarmed atop the trucks, handing their cargo of lumber, cement, and other construction material down to others on the street, from where it rapidly disappeared down side alleys and out of sight. No one seemed to be in charge of the situation— not the cowering Pakistani truck drivers, certainly not the two Americans—and Bailey took in the looting in helpless frustration.

After endless, fuming minutes, Abdullah returned with four elders of the local shura council in tow. Blandly regarding the chaotic scene, and the obviously distraught American, they politely inquired through Abdullah why they had been summoned in such haste, and what was wrong.

"Everything," barked Colonel Bailey bluntly, staring directly at each in turn.

It felt good to turn loose a little. After weeks of tact and forbearance, there did come a time when asserting himself was imperative, just as actually visiting this joint project at every step was imperative, to keep the relationship on an even keel. Only the previous day, he said curtly, he had met with the shura council about building guard stations up and down the valley. It was already agreed that the Americans would purchase construction materials, arrange delivery from the markets in Pakistan, and pay the workmen's salaries. The town council would manage the construction, ensuring that all employment was local and fairly apportioned. Together, the Afghans and Americans would pick the sites and design the posts, so they would provide immediate security for the American base and local government police posts for the valley long after the visitors were gone.

The very last thing they had agreed to yesterday, before shaking hands and hugging and saying goodbye, was regarding control of the material to be trucked from Pakistan. Warmed to his subject, Bailey slapped fingers from his right hand into his left palm to emphasize his points. The moment the trucks arrived in the village, Bailey was to be notified at the base, since he was the consignee responsible for receipt from the truckers. That did not happen; Abdullah only learned about the arrival of the convoy when he came to town for shopping! The trucks were to be guided into a walled enclosure the council had shown Bailey near the village center and secured still loaded until their contents could be inventoried. That did not happen; they sat now half empty in the middle of the public market! Lastly, Bailey and the elders were to compile an inventory as the trucks were unloaded, to make sure everything paid for was accounted for. That too did not happen; the cargo was scattered to places unknown, even as the truck drivers were demanding that Bailey sign receipts for everything. For all anyone knew, those drivers could have sold off half their consignment before crossing the border!

Catching his breath, Bailey realized that for once he had forgotten to pause frequently for Abdullah to translate. It didn't matter; he knew his voice and body language alone would make his message perfectly clear to the four elders grouped in front of him, as well as to the throng of observers that encircled them five or ten deep.

Intoning softly in Pushtu, the shura council chief, Malik Sidiki, stepped close and with his right hand began softly stroking Bailey's gray-bearded cheek—exactly as Bailey might speak to and stroke a nervous horse's neck in front of the withers. In a hot flash of anger at being mocked in front of the surrounding mob, Colonel Bailey was acutely aware of the weight of the 9mm pistol on his right hip beneath his vest, and with tunnel vision he saw Staff Sergeant Rabin tense and lean forward from his position by the wall.

In the next instant, however, Bailey flashed back thirty years, to the remote northeast of Thailand, and the broad Mekong River flowing slick and brown on the border of Laos.

Lieutenant Bailey was clean shaven then. Rivulets of sweat from the torrid heat and humidity ran down his cheeks and were consumed by the dusty yellow clay road at his feet. Towering thunderheads had been building for days, and nights of heat lightning promised, but so far cruelly withheld, relief from the burning sky and billowing dust. Bamboo huts raised on stilts, not drab mud-plastered walls, lined both sides of the village street, as if expecting a flood at any moment.

Face-to-face and straddling the front wheel of Bailey's bicycle, hands grasping the center of the handlebar, a grinning, muscular young Thai prevented movement forward or back. He and a dozen companions, like Bailey himself, were clad only in gym shorts and running shoes, yet as a group they exuded the feral, mute threat of any teen, male gang. Clearly enjoying Lieutenant Bailey's rising discomfort, they shared off one another's unintelligible comments and giggled as the leader reached into a tin can and with three dripping blue fingers streaked Bailey's forehead and cheeks with a sticky goo. Unwelcome accounts of the American Indians' treatment of prisoners by James Fennimore Cooper and others crossed his mind.

Before Bailey could react to this grinning assault into his personal space, a massive barrage of thunder rolled out of the darkening skies. Sheets of hot wind engulfed the village, rattling palm fronds and swaying huts upon their stilts. With a new sense of urgency, the young men turned from Bailey and began to hastily paint one another's faces and chests blue in similar fashion. Other villagers gathered in the street, elderly and young, male and female. From a windowsill a battery-powered boom box began pumping tinny Indian music, its ambition far beyond the capacity of its speakers. Girls joined the young men, their smiling faces more artfully painted with the same blue paste of water, talc, and dye.

The first few huge raindrops thudded into the dusty street, and village elders retreated cheerfully to the shelter of overhung roofs. The young people, a reluctant Lieutenant Bailey included, passed a jar of rice wine from hand to hand and began an impromptu dance in the middle of the street. As the scanty raindrops became a downpour, and the dancers more manic, the pummeling torrent turned their dance floor into an ankle-deep sea of mud, washed the blue talc from the dancers' faces, and soaked the cotton sarongs of the unheeding girls...

Thirty years later, Colonel Bailey still vividly recalled his day off from the war in Southeast Asia and the rare privilege of being included in that remote village's Songkran festival: their New Year celebration, the relief at the end of the long hot season, the coming of the bountiful rice-producing rains, the beginning of Southeast Asia's annual cycle of life. And he still felt a sense of nausea recalling how close he had come to breaking the neck of the young Thai astride his bicycle wheel.

Abdullah's soft voice drew Colonel Bailey back to the gritty, chaotic Afghan present. "Malik Sidiki asks you to come back tomorrow, Colonel-sa'b. You can count all the supplies together. The man who owns the walled area you saw yesterday demanded too much money when he learned that the supplies were bought by the Americans. The *shura* found a better way to store them."

Much better, I'll bet, thought Bailey. *A fair share in everyone's back rooms?* He would never know. But now that they had learned that he would show up unannounced to check, would even demand accountability, he was confident that by tomorrow the scattered materials would reassemble themselves in some central location for observation. An astonishing amount still would be mysteriously lost in the course of the project, of course, but at least now they knew they needed to buy him dinner first. "Thank you, my friend," he said as he shook the old *shura* leader's hand and hugged him warmly. "We could not succeed here without your help."

From behind the wheel of their Land Cruiser, Abdullah regarded Colonel Bailey to his right. Almost as if against his will, the ringlets of his white beard parted, and a half-smile outlined the single crooked tooth in his upper jaw. "You have lived here a long time now, Colonel-sa'b. Maybe Malik Sidiki and his companions forgot that you are an American. When an Afghan strokes the beard of an elder, it is a gesture of subordination and of supplication, of seeking favor or forgiveness. I have never seen it done to a *ferangi* before."

With tribal leader Hajji Abdul Khan Zadran, however, relations continued to sour. Over a period of days, the old warlord's importuning had become more strident, underscored by veiled threats that the tribesmen were tired of providing base security and wanted to return to their families for the Eid holiday. Finally, two nights before, Team Sergeant Sanchez had come into the base radio room and command center with the alarming news that all the

Afghan guards were missing from their posts. Interpreters hastily dispatched to Hajji Abdul's walled compound down the valley had returned with the report that he was nowhere to be found. Most ominously, radio reports had revealed the same scenario playing out at two nearby bases, both within the territories of other Zadran tribal warlords.

No shots had been fired; no hostile force could be identified. Yet the tactical and symbolic significance of this power play by the Zadrani Khans was enormous. Tribal protection of the guests (*melmestiya*, one of the cornerstones of the Pushtun code of honor) had been withdrawn. The fact that it occurred unannounced, unacknowledged, and after dark, leaving the Americans exposed, was vicious.

But not unplanned for. Master Sergeant Sanchez swiftly reorganized the night-watch roster so that a third of the Americans would be sentries on the walls with night-vision optics at all times, rather than the usual practice of one walking the wall and one awake by the radio. Bailey was both amused and grateful to note that in evident deference to his age, the tactful Team Sergeant had, unasked, assigned him the first evening hours of the watch, allowing him brief but uninterrupted sleep.

In urgent conference with the other affected bases, headquarters, and air elements at Bagram Airfield north of Kabul, Captain Maclean hammered out the details of their defensive plan and response to the Zadrani Khans. Tension in the radio room suddenly eased when a calm Texas drawl on the radio announced, "Zulu Seven One on station."

Hello, Puff, responded Colonel Bailey silently in his head. *Long time no see.* At the base only he was old enough to remember the first experimental cargo aircraft gun platform, a twin prop AC-47 mounted with a gyro-stabilized cannon and multiple machine guns, nicknamed "Puff the Magic Dragon" in Vietnam for the massive firepower it could carry and spew down on the battlefield from its slow track. Now Puff was back, but all grown up. Mounted in a four-engine Hercules AC-130 were an even more terrible array of weapons and a crew manning batteries of highly sensitive night-vision targeting equipment. High in the moonless sky hung "Spectre," their ghostly midnight guardian.

At the dawn, high flying B-52 Stratofortress bombers would take over guard duty, unseen but for lacy contrails spun in the stratosphere, poised to deliver their cargos of precision five-hundred pounders to any target designated by the men on the ground with their laser pointers. Day or night, the volume and accuracy of firepower hanging in the sky above was huge, and so was the military cost to keep it there: aircraft and crews scrambled, precious fuel expended, maintenance and support. From this serene mountain valley, however, preparing for the Eid in the first warm days of spring, it remained all but invisible, save in the relief on the faces of the isolated American team and the assurance in their step.

Hajji Abdul and his fellow Zadrani Khans must never realize that their pressure tactics had shaken the strangers or compromised their security. Down that road lay ever-escalating demands. While Pushtun honor demanded that asylum seekers be taken in and protected at all costs, this was a lean and inhospitable land, and custom required supplicants to contribute to their own upkeep. In practice, poor refugees often were reduced to near slavery and the wealthier bled dry. The American visitors were few in number and unimaginably wealthy. It must be clear it was not asylum they sought.

Nor was it tribal warfare. Any naked display of power that humiliated the khans, any hint of occupying tribal lands by force, any violent deaths by invaders' hands would inevitably provoke blood feud and the guerilla resistance that had pinned down so many invaders over the centuries in this "Graveyard of Empires." These independent mountaineers, who previously had resisted the foreign influence of al-Qa'ida and the Taliban, might instead align with them if they perceived the Americans as a common enemy. All must emerge from this impasse with honor and power intact.

Hajji Abdul and three companions stepped out of their Land Cruisers and into the red-carpeted base meeting room, each in turn shaking hands and hugging Captain Maclean and Bailey, offering the ritual Arabic greeting "Peace be upon you."

"And peace unto you," the two officers responded serenely, also in the Arabic used universally for stock phrases and religious terms despite the region's Pushtu language. Abdullah smoothly translated routine pleasantries as all settled comfortably on the plush upholstered cushions along the four walls. Cups of pale green tea appeared along with small dishes of raisins, shelled walnuts, and sweet white candies. It was universally agreed that the weather promised to be splendid for the much-anticipated Eid celebration beginning the following day.

Small talk exhausted, Captain Maclean set down his teacup and leaned forward from his cushion, legs crossed on the carpeted floor, to address Hajji Abdul and his companions seated along the opposite wall. Pausing after each one or two sentences for Abdullah to translate, he outlined his reason for their meeting and his request of Hajji Abdul and his tribesmen.

"We are strangers here, passing through your land for just a short time while we hunt the enemies who attacked our cities and killed our people... And because we are visitors, we are half blind. We can see armed groups of men, and weapons, but we are unable to recognize in advance who might be an attacker and who are just your men who live here. But we dare not let an enemy get too close, especially at night, and this is why having local men, who know the difference, to work with us is so important for all."

"For example," Captain Maclean continued, "there is a large walled compound twelve kilometers up the valley from here, on a hillside just north of the river. I do not know who lives there. It must be someone important."

Bailey resisted his urge to stare at the old brigand who sipped tea on Hajji Abdul's immediate right, whom he and Captain Maclean knew full well to be the gentleman in question. Like so many of the old Mujahedin, he wore his war decorations constantly; one leg was missing from the knee down, and the shiny scar tissue of severe burns covered one crippled hand and disappeared beneath his shirt sleeve.

"Concealed inside that compound wall is a Russian BM-21 multiple rocket launcher, a rack of launch tubes mounted on a truck, capable of firing a volley of forty Katyusha rockets at a single target in less than thirty seconds. Yesterday it was moved from its parking spot behind a building and positioned, maybe by accident, with the tubes pointing directly toward where we are sitting now. As soldiers, we cannot go into the hours of darkness with that aimed at us, where even an accidental discharge would threaten our security..."

Captain Maclean paused, and as Abdullah translated, Bailey reached into his pocket and silently pushed the "talk" button of a small walkie-talkie. In the radio room Master Sergeant Sanchez heard the static double click and keyed the mike to his radio, already set on an air control channel. "Zulu Niner One Five, this is Foxtrot Delta Three Six. Bring it on. Over."

Abdullah's translation was interrupted by a dull rumble from outside the meeting room that swiftly rose to a deafening, insane shriek. Empty teacups rattled and danced on their tin tray, jagged cracks shot across two glass window panes, and flakes of plaster spalled off walls and ceiling, exploding into little white puffs on the red carpet. Even more quickly than it had begun, the painful roar descended the scale back to a low moan and faded entirely, as the two F-16 fighter bombers, wing to wing at treetop level and almost supersonic speed, jerked their noses skyward in unison and disappeared into the cloudless sky. As if never interrupted, Abdullah removed his fingers from his ears and calmly continued, "We can always protect ourselves, of course, but only with friends and allies are we strong enough to do it gently."

In the radio room, Team Sergeant Sanchez keyed his mike again: "Zulu Niner One Five, this is Foxtrot Delta Three Six. Stand by for BDA [Battle Damage Assessment]. Two windows and three teacups destroyed, and four khans who probably wet themselves. Appreciate the help. Please drop in again soon. Over."

"Three six, this is one five. Always happy to be invited to tea. Out."

Before the evening prayer, observers high overhead reported that the offending rocket launcher up the valley had quietly spun around and returned to its former parking spot. In the radio room, Captain Maclean, Team Sergeant Sanchez, Colonel Bailey, and Abdullah glanced one to another in satisfaction.

Bailey was the first to break the silence. "Hajji Abdul received our message, and they're backing down, at least with the rocket threat. But even if the guards return, how will we know if it's really over, or if he's just biding his time until he has better odds, like any good guerilla fighter?"

After a long silence during which none of the Americans spoke, Abdulla diffidently cleared his throat. "Perhaps we will learn more from the Eid holiday tomorrow. A gift of a goat or sheep is a traditional opening of an offer for peace or a truce between two feuding families or tribes. Also, giving goats or sheep for the holiday sacrifice and feast to the poor and to those under protection is an important part of Islamic charity. If Hajji Abdul includes us in his Eid gifts, it will be a public demonstration of his wealth, power, and honor in front of the tribe, and Allah. And because the animal to be sacrificed at Eid is sacred, it could never be sent if his intentions were to attack or betray. Guards also would be nice, but I would rather have a goat, Sahibs."

A SCHOOLHOUSE FOR NURISTAN

*He was a charming old man, with that interest
in life and affairs which distinguishes the hill-
man or tribesman from the peasant, and learning was to him a real divinity.*

—Freya Stark, *The Valleys of the Assassins*

NURISTAN PROVINCE, AFGHANISTAN, 2003–2004

At not yet four in the afternoon, the sun already had disappeared over a mountain ridge to the west, and frost formed
quickly in the shadow. Where the narrow rocky road cut
sharply left, away from the river to ascend a plunging side stream,
lay the stripped and rusted shells of five armored reconnaissance
vehicles. Bailey asked Abdullah to stop their Land Rover and for
a long moment contemplated this monument to the deepest the
Soviet Army had ever penetrated into Nuristan, fifteen years before.
One chassis had been tipped up on its side. A tree grew through its

empty windows, and from a bench inside the shelter an old man gazed back at Bailey with polite curiosity as he waited for a passing ride.

Beyond, the mountain fastness had only once in history been subject to invasion. In the 1890s, the armies of Emir Abdur-Rahman had stormed up the valley to convert the aboriginal Kalash to Islam by the sword—the final region of Afghanistan to succumb and only at terrible cost to both sides. With stunning irony the great Emir had celebrated his bloody victory by renaming the region Nuristan, "Land of Enlightenment." Almost a century later, it remained remote, in topography and in thought, so much so that although the inhabitants were sympathetic toward the Great Jihad of the 1980s against the Soviets, this particular valley remained aloof from both sides, declaring themselves the independent Revolutionary Islamic State of Afghanistan, or Daulat, impartially denying Soviet passage and taxing Mujahedin supply shipments.

Bailey and his companions now carried up the valley a message of hope—of food to relieve starvation and medicines to combat epidemics, then of road upgrades, clean water, health care, electricity, and education. From Mazar-e Sharif in the north by the legendary Oxus River, to the cradle of Pushtun culture in southern Qandahar, and from hoary Herat by the Iranian border to the semitropical gateway to the Indian subcontinent at Jalalabad, the Taliban had been routed from the cities of Afghanistan. The chase now led through the remote deserts and mountains, and through the minds of their rugged inhabitants.

Thirty miles upstream, a village stair-stepped up the steep flanks of the mountain ridge on the left bank of the river, the roof of each man's house his higher neighbor's front veranda. Construction was of stone and elaborately carved timber, and the bridge that spanned the river consisted of massive timbers cantilevered from rock abutments. Even the mosque featured an ornate wooden minaret. To Bailey the architecture seemed more of the Himalaya, of Bhutan, Nepal, or Tibet, than of the Afghanistan he knew. Narrow alleyways snaked uphill, deep with mud and foot-polished ice that would not melt in the shadows until late spring.

Blanket-wrapped old men slowly gathered at a building by the river, curious but wary, assembling their *shura* council to meet the strangers. Ringing the assembly, most of the twelve-man Special Forces team that accompanied Bailey maintained a security perimeter. Initially wary, dozens of small boys peering from behind stone walls quickly caught on to Staff Sergeant Rabin's first, taunting snowballs, and delightedly launched barrages of icy missiles at the invaders. Bright flashes of color and giggles from the rooftops hinted that the village girls were not totally excluded from the momentous event.

Inside, talk and tea flowed around the overheated room. Each bearded elder in turn greeted the visitors, with profuse expressions of welcome and hospitality. Of the momentous events that had rocked first New York, and consequently Taliban dominated Afghanistan, they were well aware, due largely to the shortwave broadcasts of BBC and VOA. Several offered their sympathy to the American nation for its loss. Others remarked upon the longstanding bonds between Afghans and America, notably her support during the war against the Soviets. With each sincere but lengthy welcoming speech, Abdullah's translation grew briefer, until it became a simple "More greetings."

Seated upon a floor deep in layers of red and brown wool carpets, Bailey sipped his tea and accepted a sugar cookie proffered by his neighbor on his right. A sudden, urgent itching around his ankles and up his legs revealed that humans were not the only occupants of the council house carpet, and the elders' kind invitation to bunk down inside for the night lost its initial appeal. Finally each graybeard had had his say, and all turned expectantly toward Bailey for his response, for an answer to the question all had been too polite to ask. Why had the Americans come to their remote valley?

Pausing frequently to allow Abdullah to translate, Bailey thanked the assembly effusively for their welcome, commenting that he and his companions had journeyed to this remote location confident of finding Afghan hospitality, and security at their hearth. He invoked the historical bonds between their peoples, deliberately mentioning his pride and privilege in having his own bit part in the Great Jihad of the 1980s. Finally he got to the point he had traveled so far to make. Change was coming to Afghanistan; the modern world was asserting itself again after decades of barbarism. The new government in Kabul and its American allies intended to bring this change to every tribe and village, no matter how remote.

It would not come easily in regions as remote as this, of course, as his listeners knew better than anyone. The mountain barriers were formidable, government resources were limited, and the old enemies were in retreat but not yet vanquished. Bailey and his companions were but the first emissaries, come to introduce themselves, to talk about the new order, to see the difficulties—but primarily to listen, to learn firsthand from the people of this far mountain valley their needs and wants, their hopes for the future. If all went well, they would build a plan together, so that when help arrived, it would bring the best of the modern world, without harming their pristine land, their heritage, or their freedoms.

The first assistance efforts, Bailey emphasized, would be miniscule. Demands throughout Afghanistan for available resources were enormous in the wake of decades of warfare, and this valley was as remote as any in the land. The long and difficult road up the valley could support nothing larger than a pickup truck, and it traversed the territories of rival, equally needy, tribes. The imperative, therefore, was for this council to identify their most desperate, primary needs, and to help plan with the Americans for a first small shipment of aid during the winter months. The Americans and the Afghan government might find supplies, might even find funds to hire trucks and drivers, but only the elders knew the true needs of their community, how to arrange reliable transport, and how to deal with the other tribes through whose territory the shipments must pass.

Based on their experiences in other war-ravaged towns and villages throughout Afghanistan, the Americans had come to find out how many families were in dire need of food to avoid starvation during the long winter or heating oil to survive the cold. Were there epidemic or endemic diseases that required medicines to prevent winter deaths? And, of course, was the region under further threat from the Taliban and their al-Qa'ida allies?

Bailey paused and turned the floor over to Captain Maclean, who dutifully repeated his team's gratitude for the elders' hospitality, their hopes for Afghanistan and for Nuristan, their desire to be the spearhead of a bright future. Bailey leaned back against the hard, round pillows that lined the walls, smiled inwardly at the new brevity of Abdullah's translations, and unobtrusively scratched the fleabites on his ankles.

When Captain Maclean in turn ceased speaking, animated discussion broke out among the elders, exchanging salvos in incomprehensible Nuristani dialect across the carpet. Now they made no effort to direct their remarks to Abdullah. This was their private caucus, and Abdullah discretely directed his attention to his tea and to making conversation in English with the two Americans.

"Honored American guests, we are very grateful that you travel so far to speak with us." The white-bearded speaker, dressed in crisp, brown linen shirt and trousers with a darker wool vest, sat against the far wall, directly opposite Bailey and Captain Maclean. He waved Abdullah to silence and addressed the two in unexpected, although halting, English.

"Please accept our humble hospitality and gratitude for your offer to help us. As you said, we are far from cities. Now it is even farther than before, under the king. Everything you speak about, we need. Winter will be hard. Many families will be hungry before spring comes and crops grow. Some of our very old people will become sick and die in the winter...and some of the very young. It will be as God wills.

"But, I say to you, that is not because of the Taliban or the war. It is the way life always has been. Our humble request is for you to help us with the thing that we most need, that we could not get during all the years of the wars—education for our children. There is no money for books or to pay teachers. The school for boys, built just across the river by the king, is small and old and falls down. It is now a mosque school, a *madrassa*, not a regular school, because some money came from the Saudis. For the girls we have nothing. One or two women teach in their homes, but many, many girls have no place to learn at all. So this is the help we humbly request from our American friends: schools, especially one for the girls. This is the way we can become part of the new Afghanistan, and the modern world."

```
FROM: SPECIAL OPERATIONS COMMAND/KABUL
(SOC/K)

SUBJECT: REQUEST FOR SCHOOL AID

1. DO NOT, REPEAT NOT, COMMIT TO SCHOOL-
BUILDING INITIATIVE. PROGRAM FUNDS ARE
RESTRICTED TO WINTER EMERGENCY AID AND
LOCATING AND FIXING HOSTILE ELEMENTS.
```

```
2. SCHOOL SUPPORT/CONSTRUCTION IS A
FOLLOW-ON MISSION FOR MILITARY CIVIL
AFFAIRS, USAID AND NGOS—NOT SPECIAL
OPERATIONS FORCES. ASSURE VILLAGE ELDERS
THAT WE HAVE FORWARDED THEIR REQUEST
TO US EMBASSY, KABUL, FOR PASSAGE TO
APPROPRIATE AGENCIES.

3. MAKE ARRANGEMENTS, PER OPERATIONS
ORDER, FOR DELIVERY OF EMERGENCY FOOD,
MEDICINES, FUEL OIL, THEN RETURN TO
BASE.
```

Watching the blocky green letters scroll across the dark screen of his satellite-linked laptop, Captain Maclean swore under his breath, then turned in exasperation to his "special advisor." "How the hell can we ask these guys to decide what they need, then blow them off and just send what those rear-echelon geniuses already decided was good for them? It's like HQ's been captured by Democrats," he sputtered.

"I can't tell them we've passed their request on to bureaucrats in Kabul. They'll know what bullshit that is before Abdullah even translates. Five years at Columbia, and I didn't feel a bit like the smartest guy in the room last night. Or the cleanest, for that matter. Isn't there someone you can go to? Or, we do have contingency funds. Couldn't we just drop a thousand on them for teachers' salaries or something?"

"To live outside the law, you must be honest," Bailey chanted in a nasal monotone. "You young pups probably don't remember the great Bobby Dylan, singing 'Absolutely Sweet Marie' at Newport in sixty-eight. Anyway, there's a reason we're called *Special* Forces, and we're allowed to roll around this far from the flagpole with enough guns to start a new religion and rucksacks full of money. Unfortunately that's because we carry out orders, even the hard ones. Now that we've been told 'no,' we're pretty much screwed–at least for now.

"I'm kicking myself; none of us saw a request like this coming. So Hindquarters is right, for once...no money programmed for this purpose, no supplies in the pipeline. And no time for us to wait around for a change from on high, even if the Old Man wants to support us. Hang out too long in one place in this country and trouble will always show up.

"So here's what we need to do. We'll be completely up front with the shura council, admit no one anticipated or prepared for supporting education this early, tell them right now we're limited to the supplies in the pipeline. But when we tell them the request has been forwarded to Kabul, we'll add that you and I, as American military officers, personally commit to the elders here to return to tackle this problem with them. We'll be clear that we're under military orders—and in a war—so it's not entirely in our hands, but they'll understand. It's that personal commitment that will be meaningful to them, not some promises about Kabul. Of course, we have to mean it."

Seven months later the river roared bank-full with milky glacier melt beneath the wooden cantilever bridge, and a heavy scent of pine seemed to flow down from the forested hillsides above the town. Higher yet, snowfields gleamed in the June sunlight. Across the river, Bailey and Captain Maclean watched a seemingly endless line of villagers, predominantly men carrying babies or leading small children by the hand, pass into a walled courtyard, where the two medics from Captain Maclean's team conducted a free medical clinic. Yesterday, the day the team had arrived, most of the patients had been from the town, but today many were from villages as far away as a twelve-hour walk up the valley.

Abdullah brought the attention of the two officers back to the rectangle of roughly leveled rocky ground, outlined by a low stone wall less than a meter high, immediately in front of them. One soot-blackened corner, with several half-burned logs and a pile of rusty cans, gave the place an air of neglect and desertion even in the crystal sunshine. This was, Abdullah explained, the site chosen by the shura council for the first-ever school for girls in the valley.

Immediately after the winter snows melted and the road down the valley opened in the Spring, a man had arrived from Chitral. He was from a charity and development organization, he said, an NGO, and he would help them build their school. The village elders told Abdullah they were astonished that the message to the powers in far-off Kabul actually had borne fruit. Local craftsmen and merchants eagerly agreed to contracts for materials and labor, and work commenced as the Chitrali NGO representative snapped pictures on a small digital camera. After three days, he drove off down the valley, bound for Kabul to pick up the money to pay off the contracts and buy additional supplies. He never returned, and now the half-finished foundation stood, a monument to betrayed faith and idealism, to workers unpaid and merchants without materials or means to purchase more.

"This is happening all over Afghanistan," Abdullah explained vehemently. Bailey had never before seen the old man so angry. The long white ringlets of his beard quivered, and his hooded black eyes flashed, like a very wrathful Moses about to strike Pharaoh's army. "Villagers hear the promises of millions of dollars in aid from the West over the BBC and VOA, so of course they believe this is a true program. But miscreants like this one come, make promises, go to Kabul with the contracts and photos of make-believe projects, sometimes letters and petitions from the local shura. They receive money from government agencies and non-governmental organizations, put it in their pockets, and disappear. True Muslims do not steal from the poor like this. These are *dacoits*, common criminals.

"The worst thing is not the stolen money but the stolen faith. In village after village after village, Afghans learn to doubt the government and the NGOs and the promises from the West. Colonel-sa'b, why do they just sit in Kabul and give away the money and never check what is being done with it? The wahabbis, the Arabs, the Taliban are out here; people see their faces; and when they say they will build a school, or burn one down, they do it.

"Captain-sa'b, Colonel-sa'b, the reason they greeted us in friendship when we arrived yesterday was that you two are the only government officers, Afghan or American, who have ever returned here for more than one short visit, who ever came back from far away to see what really happens to them. Even if the news about their school is bad, they respect the promise you have fulfilled."

Abdullah ceased speaking, flushed with emotion and perhaps embarrassment about lecturing the two officers. His audience exchanged glances.

"Gloves off?" suggested Captain Maclean.

"Cry havoc and let slip the dogs of PSYWAR," responded Bailey.

FROM: PSYCHOLOGICAL OPERATIONS STAFF/
KABUL (POS/K)

SUBJECT: INDICATORS OF ARAB PRESENCE/
INFLUENCE.

1. COMMUNITY ANALYSTS READ WITH INTEREST
YOUR INTELLIGENCE REPORT (INTELREP 001)
OF SAUDI/WAHABBI MONEY AND INFLUENCE
ENTERING THE REGION FROM PAKISTAN.

2. FOLLOWING TALKING POINTS ARE PROVIDED
FOR FURTHER REPORTING, IF POSSIBLE:

A) PER INTELREP, VILLAGERS TRAVELING
OVER THE DAULAT PASS, DIRECTLY
NORTH FROM YOUR LOCATION, REPORTED
TENSE ATMOSPHERICS AND RUMORS OF
ARAB PRESENCE IN THE TRADING TOWN
OF CHAMICHU, PAKISTAN. OTHER ALL-
SOURCE REPORTING INDICATES THE RECENT
PRESENCE IN CHAMICHU OF AN EGYPTIAN
AND A SOMALI. CAN YOUR SOURCES
IDENTIFY ANY OF THE FOREIGNERS? WERE
THERE VISIBLE BODYGUARDS OR OTHER
INDICATIONS OF HIGH-VALUE TARGETS
(HVTS)?

B) CAN SOURCES COMMENT ON POPULAR
REACTIONS TO ARAB FUNDING OF THE
MADRASSA? ARE THERE OTHER INDICATORS OF
OUTSIDE INFLUENCE?

"Good cast," said Bailey as Captain Maclean hit the "send" button with his response. "There should be a lunker looking over your bait already."

FROM: PSYCHOLOGICAL OPERATIONS STAFF/
KABUL (POS/K)

SUBJECT: PROPOSED PSYCHOLOGICAL
OPERATION

1. PSYCHOLOGICAL OPERATIONS STAFF/
KABUL HAS REVIEWED YOUR RESPONSE TO
COMMUNITY QUERIES (INTELREP 002) AND
PROPOSES THE FOLLOWING PSYCHOLOGICAL
OPERATION.

2. BACKGROUND: PER REPORTING, HOSTILE
INFLUENCE OPERATIONS TO DATE SEEM
LIMITED TO PROMOTING MADRASSAS AND
TEACHING RADICAL ISLAM, MAKING THE
BATTLEFIELD THE NEXT GENERATION—FOR
THE MOMENT. IF UNCHECKED, EXPERIENCE
IN OTHER AREAS INDICATES THEY MIGHT
ESCALATE TO CHALLENGING LOCAL LEADERS'
AND SHURA COUNCIL'S AUTHORITIES, FIRST
WITH PROPAGANDA AND THEN WITH ARMED
COERCION. AT THIS POINT THERE IS NO
REPORTING TO DETERMINE WHETHER THE
REPORTED DISSAPPEARANCE OF THE NGO WAS
SIMPLE FRAUD OR THREATS AND/OR DIRECT
ACTION BY HOSTILE ELEMENTS. PER YOUR

INTELREP, POPULATION AND LEADERS ARE
PREDICTABLY RELUCTANT TO CHALLENGE AND
RESIST ESTABLISHMENT OF MADRASSAS, AS
LONG AS THERE IS NO OTHER CHOICE FOR
EDUCATION OF THEIR YOUTH.

3. PSYCHOLOGICAL OPERATION: POS/K
THEREFORE DIRECTS ESTABLISHING,
UNDER GOVERNING COUNCIL LEADERSHIP,
TRADITIONAL SCHOOLS TO PROVIDE AN
ALTERNATIVE TO RADICAL RELIGIOUS
INSTRUCTION AND TO REINFORCE TRIBAL
SHURA AUTHORITY. FUNDS NOT TO EXCEED 1.2
MILLION PAKISTANI RUPEES [USD 20,000]
HAVE BEEN ALLOCATED.

4. OBJECTIVES: PRIMARY OBJECTIVE IS
TO INNOCULATE THE POPULATION IN YOUR
VICINITY AGAINST RADICAL INFLUENCE
OPERATIONS. THIS MAY IN TURN ENHANCE
REPORTING ON THE AL-QA'IDA TARGET.
ADDITIONALLY, IT MAY FORCE AL-QA'IDA
TO SEEK A MORE LUCRITIVE TARGET AREA,
RENDERING THEM MORE VULNERABLE TO
DETECTION AND NEUTRALIZATION AS THEY
MOVE INTO UNFAMILIAR TERRITORY.

5. SUBMIT FIELD COMMANDER'S CONCEPT OF OPERATIONS (CONOP) AND IMPLEMENT ASAP UTILIZING CONTINGENCY FUNDS ON HAND.

In the far corner of a dim, cavernous room, a five-man band beat out a raucous tune on drums and oddly shaped stringed instruments. Urged on by laughing comrades, men in turn strutted to the center of the dance floor and performed whirling, lunging solos to the insistent tempo. Crowding all four walls were what seemed to be all the males of the town (save perhaps the *mullah* from the *madrassa*), blowing smoke toward the ceiling, cheering the dancers, throwing rupee notes onto the floor to reward particularly flamboyant performances. The small red and green notes flew like confetti as Staff Sergeant Rabin claimed the floor and threw himself into a stomping, spinning break dance.

When a brief rest for the band reduced the din, Bailey leaned back against his red wool cushion, idly scratched his ankle, and raised an insulated aluminum travel mug of sour-smelling, milky local wine to Captain Maclean, Abdullah, and the white-bearded shura spokesman. The great Emir Abdur-Rahman's conquest may not have been as complete as he had imagined.

"Here's to the girls of the countryside," Colonel Bailey toasted. "May they all grow up to be doctors, none of them lawyers." In a quiet aside to Captain Maclean, he continued, "In all the best psychological operations, everyone believes he's the PSYOPer, and no one realizes he's the target. I'm sure POS/K realizes that as well."

THE LEGEND OF
THE BLUE ICE CUBE

*{Hasan, The Old Man of the Mountain} lived
there {in the fortress of Alamut, 1091–1125 AD}
with his secret garden and his devoted Fedawis
around him, and combined assassination with
the liberal arts in his efficient way.*

—Freya Stark, *The Valleys of the Assassins*

KABUL, AFGHANISTAN, 2004

"It's over. First came Kellogg Brown and Root contractors, arriving on the Air Force transports from Tashkent into Bagram, setting up mess halls and bunkered compounds for the regular troops. Then Judge Advocate General and State Department lawyers, and now the first visiting congressional delegation [CODEL in Statespeak]. Afghanistan is a war zone, damn it! Soldiers are fighting and dying. Tourists shouldn't be here."

The cue ball clicked around a felt pool table, punctuated by exaggerated groans and shouts of triumph. Cirrus streamers of blue cigar smoke drifted beneath a ceiling of camouflage net. On walls of unfinished marine plywood hung trophy weapons: an ancient jezail with its absurdly curved stock from the tribal gun factories in Dara Adam Khel across the Durand Line; a new and highly polished Soviet sniper rifle; AK-47s pimped up with brass tacks and shiny red and blue plastic tassels. Scrawled in magic marker between the weapons by sometimes unsteady hands were dozens of dates and nicknames of passers through, along with slogans, unit and team logos, and quotes:

The Wolf Pack, Dec '01 – Feb '02
Lobo Six

Team Raven: Blacker than Black

If you're gonna be stupid,
you gotta be strong.

"We fight not for wealth or honor or glory, but only and alone for freedom which no good man surrenders but with his life."

– Robert the Bruce, 1314 A.D.

"Religion-freedom-vengeance-what you will.
A word's enough to raise mankind to kill.
– Lord Byron

"When everyone is dead the Great Game is finished.
Not before."
– The Babu

"I hear you, America hears you, and soon the people who did this will hear you."
– G. Bush, 17 Sept. '01

Prominent on one wall was a head-on sketch of a medevac helicopter, surrounded by the first name signatures of its crew. Immediately below was the classic radio transmission calling it in not long ago: *"Gunfire to the east, winds calm, land at your own risk."* Colonel Bailey had been elsewhere, but he vividly remembered that long night. Leaning back in his armchair, he regarded the speaker and the half dozen others talking shop. "Things are changing," he agreed. "Some of the Wild West days are over. Maybe now would be a good time to tell The Legend of the Blue Ice Cube."

Not so long ago, there was a different war here, although a lot of the characters looked the same then as now. But, in those days Kabul was the headquarters for The Bad Guys, while The Good Guys operated from the east, beyond the Durand Line. And, you should know, at the time I will describe, that war had been going on a long time. It was well beyond the money, guns, and lawyers stage. For a secret war, it was remarkably popular in Washington, Texas, and parts of the Mountain West, so with the regularity and inevitability of the tides, with each biweekly British Air flight between London and Islamabad ebbed and flowed a flood of Banana Republicans.

Some actually did arrive in brand-new safari suits, photographers' vests, and chukka boots, right out of the Banana Republic store that then sat on the corner of Wisconsin and M in Georgetown. Here they were, on the new frontier of freedom, to stare down the muzzles of the commie invaders. There were CODELs of course. Politically appointed undersecretaries from State and DOD. A few just rich and politically connected. And exactly like you just did, we all complained about these *"tourists."*

Every last one of them wanted face time with The Old Man, of course, since he was running things, from his separate, fenced-off building behind the rose garden at the sprawling American Embassy compound in Islamabad. Our part of things, that is; there were other special offices at the Pakistani Army Headquarters in Rawalpindi, the Saudi Embassy in the Diplomatic Quarter, and so on.

Now, The Old Man should have been even more impatient with these intruders than we were, as busy as he was, and as gruff. But no, you would have thought he was a Georgetown hostess. Each group of official visitors was invited for a gala cocktail party the first evening after their arrival, and they felt like they finally had met the last Viceroy.

He had a big house not far from the diplomatic quarter, with spacious gardens inside its privacy wall, all set up for gracious entertaining. Staff like it was still the Raj: cooks, waiters, busboys, gardeners and gate guards, even a four-man band playing typical Pushtun instruments and all dressed up in Afridi finery. All of this was presided over by his majordomo, an old graybeard, immaculate in red embroidered cap and vest, long-tailed shirt and baggy trousers, and even red slippers with up-curled toes. He was the only man I ever met who could carry off those "harem slippers." Trust me, no one so much as snickered at that old cutthroat. His real name was Mohammed, but to me he always will be Punjab, like Daddy Warbucks's right-hand man in *Little Orphan Annie*.

"Sure they're a pain in the ass," the Old Man explained to us once. "What you young pups don't remember is how much worse it is to deal with politicians during an *un*popular war."

But his uncharacteristic tolerance did have its limits. Congressmen who showed up ignorant of the facts and issues, who only came for bragging rights with their constituents and backers. And demanding staffers, trying to throw their members' weight around to get special treatment for themselves. So legend has it that the Old

Man had a secret hand signal to point out these types to Punjab at the welcome parties, and they soon would be served a very special cocktail. The best Scotch obtainable from the embassy commissary, over ice cubes from a single, blue ice cube tray, stored separately in the freezer and refilled as needed by Punjab from the public spigot at the "Christian slum" in Rawalpindi.

Any number of these visitors disappeared into their rooms at their five-star hotels, not to emerge, much less bother the Old Man, until their return flights. None of us had the nerve to ask The Old Man about it of course. Once, I did hear him comment unsympathetically when told of an ill visitor, "If sickness is weakness, then death is the ultimate wimp-out."

Still, the whole thing is probably apocryphal. But like our friends the war correspondents used to say, hanging over the bar at the American Club in Peshawar, it's a story too good to check.

THIS TROUBLESOME PRIEST

*...and I rode on sadly in the darkness,
weighed down by the cruelty of Asia...*

—Freya Stark, *The Valleys of the Assassins*

AFGHANISTAN, 2008

Τhe old *mullah* paused, teacup in midair, as a muffled call to prayer, *"Allaaaa-hu Akbar,"* rumbled from deep within the folds of the silk sash around his ample waist. "Excuse me," he murmured in his quiet voice, a sly grin almost buried within his luxurious white beard. "This might be Allah calling," he explained as he dug out the chanting cell phone.

As al-Qa'ida and the Taliban sought to impose their ruthless seventh-century vision of Islam on his homeland, Mulawi Shafiq was determined to meet them head-on in the twenty-first century. From an ancient mosque in the heart of Kandahar, the cultural and religious locus of the Pushtun nation as well as the birthplace of the

Taliban movement, his voice and teachings rang out in concentric circles. Hundreds attended his Friday sermons that challenged the radical pronouncements of al-Qa'ida and the Taliban, then spilled out into the crowded alleys and bazaars to discuss his dangerous message of moderation.

Over the airways his popular radio talk show, *The Mullah Answers*, fielded questions from the city's youth, providing guidance for living according to the true tenets of Islam and countering the constant Islamist drumbeat. Drop boxes in city mosques and tea houses to collect these questions in writing had all been blown up within days of the radio program's initial airing, so now submissions flowed in by the hundreds via anonymous voice-mail and text messages. This provided safety for the questioners, but not so for the old *mullah*, who faced daily threats with a characteristic Afghan blend of reckless courage and fatalism.

He did quit once, and none who knew him held it against him or questioned his courage. His oldest son, six-year-old Husain, had come into the house carrying an improvised bomb that had been left by their gate onto the street, wrapped with a green ribbon like a holiday gift. No one ever discovered why it did not explode in Husain's hands. Shaken and depressed, Mulawi Shafiq had dropped out of public view and even cut himself off from his worried friends. Four months later he reemerged just as abruptly to resume his former activities, more resolved than ever that his sons and daughters should inherit an Afghanistan free of the scourges of intolerance and violence.

Now again the old man reveled in the popular response to his radio program and brimmed with ideas to broaden its scope. He had begun a new regional effort as well, a broad network of text messages to cell phones announcing extremist atrocities as they occurred and succinctly explaining how each was an insult to the true teachings of Islam before the Taliban propagandists could disseminate their messages of hate.

The scope of Mulawi Shafiq's scholarship and influence were not confined within text messages, nor within dust-, sun-, and opium-drenched southern Afghanistan. In collaboration with likeminded imams in Cairo and Medina, he recently had composed a series of exhaustively researched and finely reasoned lectures concerning al-Qa'ida's tactic of suicide bombing. Step by damning step, they spelled out the Koran's prohibitions against suicide, its condemnation of the killing of innocents and believers, and the guilt shared by those who teach, advocate, or finance such un-Islamic acts. Step by damning step, they debunked the rationales put forward by "Imam Rashid," the alias of al-Qa'da's chief proponent of self-destruction.

No photographs existed of Imam Rashid nor any hint of his real name or background. His voice was seldom heard on the public airways or on the jihadist Internet sites. He was known to frequent al-Qa'ida's militant training camps, instructing the most fanatic recruits. His CDs, in the pure Arabic of the Egyptian elite, extolling violent jihad against believers and unbelievers, the innocent and the guilty, male, female and child alike, circulated from hand to hand in the radical *madrassa* schools of the Islamic world. So using Imam Rashid's own words alone, Mulawi Shafiq and his allies demonstrated Rashid's misrepresentation of the sacred texts, his lack of religious education or erudition, and his unqualified presumption

in issuing decrees on religious subjects. With devastating argu-
ments, the so-called imam was proved to be not an Islamic scholar
but the apostate disciple of a cult of death.

From the narrow platform of a minaret high above the city,
Colonel Bailey regarded the scene below and cursed as he recalled that
last meeting with his old friend. Now, bloody flagstones and a Holy
Koran torn through by a high-power rifle round bore silent witness
to Mulawi Shafiq's final Friday Prayer. "Assassination," Bailey had
said once in a lecture at Fort Bragg, "is the sincerest form of flattery."
Now those words seemed glib, cheap. There were no HESCO bun-
kers here, no growling Humvees, no body-armored riflemen with
pumped and tattooed biceps. This dusty, shrapnel-riddled mosque
was the real front line, and the old scholar/soldier had made the ultimate sacrifice in the war vying for the soul of Islam.

Only that challenge and humiliation of Imam Rashid could
have led to this final chapter of his old friend's life, Colonel Bailey
believed. On the day following the rifle fire that had ripped through
the open window of his mosque to end the life of the holy man,
hundreds gathered to bury their revered teacher and tribesman
according to the laws of Islam. In the center of the courtyard, just
as the crowd lifted the sheet-wound remains of Mulawi Shafiq to
their shoulders for the funeral procession, a young man detonated
his lethal vest of plastic explosives and nails.

The cult of death had perfected itself. The worshipers of death
now attacked the dead themselves.

Unbidden, a hot flush of anger consumed Bailey—at Mulawi Shafiq, for his reckless courage; at himself, for his failure to somehow protect the old *mullah* or persuade him to temper his rhetoric; and, strangely last, at the blasphemers who committed these atrocities in the name of religion. One way or another, he would identify and find Imam Rashid. For the moment, however he needed distance and time for grief.

At first a barely perceptible throbbing from the north, the huge, lumbering form of the aircraft seemed to materialize suddenly overhead, a roaring black outline against the curtain of stars in the Afghan night, surrounded by a sparkling halo where flinty sand flew up into the thrashing rotor. Colonel Bailey spun and hunched his shoulders as the gritty blast washed over him. When the roar of the engine reduced to an idle, he turned and stumbled clumsily across the dark, rubble-strewn landing zone to clamber aboard.

A moon-bright cascade of icy rock and snowfields plunged earthward, framed by the open helicopter door, seeming almost to brush the muzzle of the protruding machine gun. Inside the darkened aircraft, the gunner was a barely visible silhouette, backlit by the pale glow of instrument lights. In bulky parka and shooter's mittens, helmet mounted in front with the beak-like protrusion of night-vision goggles and behind with a block of batteries to counterbalance, eye sockets glowing luminescent green from the optics, he hunched behind his weapon like some nightmare pterodactyl.

Colonel Bailey slid his backpack beneath his feet to insulate them from the frigid aluminum floor, his carbine wedged muzzle down between his knees, and willed the memory of Mulawi Shafiq's chanting cell phone to recede like the mountainside. He was not cold yet, but he knew the chill would seep in bone-deep, through his mountain parka, his boots and fleece cap, as he sat immobile and the flight went on and the punishing high-altitude wind swirled through the open doors.

The roaring, lurching helicopter flight transitioned to the soft hum of air conditioning, muted lights, and plush reclining seats of a mammoth Airbus soaring through the skies of Central Asia, bound for Europe and across the Atlantic. More than ever before, Bailey needed this transition, a dimly lit tunnel between worlds cutting him off from phone and radio and companions, from the urgent demands and sometimes unbearable horrors behind, and from the plunge ahead into the chaotic foreign land of family and Christmas season.

MY FERAL UNCLE

A human being should be able to change a diaper,
plan an invasion, butcher a hog, conn a ship, design
a building, write a sonnet, balance accounts, build
a wall, set a bone, comfort the dying, take orders,
give orders, cooperate, act alone, solve equations,
analyze a new problem, pitch manure, program
a computer, cook a tasty meal, fight efficiently, die
gallantly. Specialization is for insects.

—Robert A. Heinlein

UNITED STATES, 2008

Mom's brother has visited a couple of times a year ever since I can remember. He brings the most wonderful presents, and teaches me interesting, important things, and drives Mom nuts—which makes everything even more fun. To me he's my Uncle Akaa, except that's redundant of course, since "Akaa" means "Uncle" in Pushtunistan, which isn't really a country, but where

Uncle Akaa spends a lot of time between visits. I'm a little vague on the details.

Except when he's here, Mom calls Uncle Akaa "your feral uncle" or "my feral brother." It really bugs her that he doesn't have a "responsible" job, or do other "respectable" stuff. She says he joined the Green Berets right after college to avoid getting a real job, and because they'd let him travel around the world, living outdoors, jumping out of airplanes, and having adventures. Once, Dad pointed out that Uncle Akaa actually was drafted into the Army, like almost everyone else during Vietnam. Sure, said Mom, even shriller than usual, but none of his classmates seemed to have any trouble getting graduate school exceptions, or at worst serving a couple of years on a Navy ship or something, then moving right on to Wall Street or politics. Dad resumed his usual silence.

Mom wouldn't let it go, though. According to her, after twenty years of "underpaid adventuring," just when Uncle Akaa was in line for prestige positions as a general officer, he abruptly retired. All so he could go overseas again, as an advisor with no rank at all, in places with no indoor plumbing. Dad continued his silence.

Uncle Akaa's pet name for me is "Gingat", which I adore and which especially rattles Mom's cage, since it means "dung beetle" in that Pushtu language that is special between us, which isn't a proper name for a "young lady." I guess I should explain how I became "Gingat."

The summer I was twelve, Uncle Akaa arrived to visit, driving an old pickup truck, towing a rusty trailer with a horse inside.

Leaving the horse issue aside for a moment, it was clear Mom was annoyed having that rig parked in the driveway all the time where the neighbors could see it, but Uncle Akaa didn't seem to notice. Anyway, back to the horse, which can't really be ignored for long. Especially when you're twelve. Inside the trailer was the most adorable pinto gelding ever. He was white with big black splotches all over, his mane hung down the side of his neck almost a foot, and his big brown eyes were the size of soup plates. His name was Abu Khairan, Uncle Akaa announced, and Abu Khairan was going to teach me horsemanship. Horsemanship, it turned out later, consists mostly of riding and mucking, but with some other important stuff thrown in.

First, though, Mom and Dad had to come to terms with Abu Khairan. Watching Uncle Akaa play Mom like a violin was observing a maestro at work. He opened with birthday gifts for me—box after box of clothes. My least favorite things to get at Christmas and birthdays, but...there was a trim, tailored hunt coat, midnight blue with a black velvet collar. A black velvet-covered helmet. A couple of ratcatcher shirts in pastel shades, and canary riding britches. Somehow he had managed to get everything in exactly my size, but before long I caught on that they weren't really for me, but for Mom.

Sure enough, her initial volley about how dangerous and expensive and dirty horses were soon tapered off. She began to drift off into some vision of herself standing at the rail at the annual horse show downtown, me parading around the ring, back straight, horse and boots gleaming, blue ribbon placed on the side of Abu Khairan's bridle by the judges, loudspeakers announcing our names. All the snobby boarding school girls and their parents clapping. Reluctantly. To this day, I don't believe Mom knows that "Abu Khairan" translates as "Father of Dirt."

Dad helped out too, pointing out that horses are pretty much a girl's sport, unlike most of the tomboy things I like. And he remarked that girls with horses to occupy them didn't seem to become so boy-crazy. (Which I was certainly not. But, if it would help get me that wonderful pinto in Uncle Akaa's trailer I might try it for a while.)

Later, at the barn with just me and Abu Khairan, Uncle Akaa continued the discussion. Horses are for girls, of course, especially these days, he said, but there's a few thousand years of history between men and horses too. Warhorses, cow horses, farm horses, cart horses: heroes and workers. Back when the Brits had an empire, and standards to maintain, training in horsemanship was required of all commissioned military officers and princes of the blood. That was for the same reason that Abu Khairan had come here to teach me: horses have no respect for rank or reputation. Nobody tells them whether you are a princess or a stable hand, owner or servant. Whatever you get back from them, whether it's being dumped on your ass in a mud puddle, winning medals, or a lifetime of devotion, will be solely the result of your individual interaction with this huge, mysterious combination of muscle and instinct.

Besides, he added with a grin, this is the only major sport where guys and girls compete head-to-head on an even basis. You may see mostly girls at local competitions, but if you want an Olympic medal, you're going to have to go through a lot of big, tough guys, and just as many little, tough girls. If that's what you want. If you want it enough.

But first, like I said before, it turned out that riding is only part of Uncle Akaa's horsemanship thing. At the stable, there were hands to feed and turn the horses in and out to pasture, clean the stalls, and help the visiting blacksmith and vet. The boarders, including a good many of the boarding school girls, would just show up in their clean tight britches and designer tops, saddle up, and ride their dressage and jumping lessons.

That wasn't nearly good enough for Uncle Akaa. At least until school started again, the stable staff would do nothing for Abu Khairan. I was solely responsible, "from beginning to end," as he put it. And for the rest of my life, even if I had help, I would understand how much work it is to be responsible for another living creature and how it must be done.

"Here's your real birthday present—your very own pitchfork, Gingat. Start at the back then work your way up to the bit."

And the guns! I need to explain the guns. Actually, officially it was just one gun, my sixteenth-birthday present. A sleek, over & under, twenty-gauge shotgun from James Purdey and Sons of London, with their scaled-down "lady's stock," all checkered Turkish walnut and pungent oiled steel, nestled in green velvet inside its custom leather and brass-buckled case. "Of course," Uncle

Akaa explained guilelessly, "when she's invited to her first country weekend, she'll need to know how to shoot the grouse and not the gamekeepers." I could just feel Mom visualizing me dressed head to toe in tweeds.

Well, there weren't any grouse, and no tweeds, at the local firing range where Uncle Akaa took me to learn to shoot. One unpainted cinderblock building way back in the woods, sometimes a couple of redneck civilians, and a whole lot of state troopers, sheriff's deputies, and chewing tobacco. You learned quick to keep track of your own Coke bottle! They all thought it was really cool that a girl was there shooting and cleaned up their language and spoiled me outrageously. That was the best part of all. Along with the idea that Uncle Akaa brought me there and trusted me.

In a different way, the cops all seemed to find Uncle Akaa pretty cool too. They were always showing him their new guns, and asking his advice, and telling him about their adventures in the military and as cops, and calling him "Sir." It didn't seem to bother any of them that he had retired without becoming a general.

One day we drove up, and two armored trucks were there, and a dozen big guys in black uniforms, combat boots, helmets, and bulletproof vests with "SWAT" in big letters across the back. I thought for sure Uncle Akaa would make a U-turn and leave them the range for the day, but no. He pulled up right beside their trucks, walked over, and started chatting with the captain. The rest of them just sort of milled around, fiddling with the carbines hung muzzle down from slings over their necks, and I felt like they were all staring at me, although since all of them wore mirrored sunglasses, who knew? So I slipped on the amber, wrap-around shooter's glasses Uncle Akaa had given me, leaned against his rusty old pickup, and pretended I was wearing black body armor too.

Before you know it, they had broken out all kinds of foreign guns. I could recognize the AK-47; there was a machine gun with a folding bipod; and there were all sorts of pistols. Uncle Akaa was teaching them a class: how to see if they were loaded and safe to fire if you picked them up in the street, how to shoot them, how to take them apart for cleaning. They were hanging on to every word Uncle Akaa said and not paying the slightest attention to me anymore.

But then at the end, when the rest were cleaning all the guns, the captain and Uncle Akaa took me over to the firing point and let me fire one of their snub-nosed black automatic carbines. It's not a bit like it looks on TV, and it was probably a good thing that they were standing close enough to grab me the first time I flipped the lever to full auto and pulled the trigger. Good thing there weren't any airplanes overhead too. Pretty soon I got the hang of it, though, and could rip off three- and four-shot groups right into the man-size paper target of a big, scary dude with tattoos and a knife. Mom would have had a coronary if I'd told her we weren't shooting sporting clays or Scottish grouse, and the guys in my class who come in all puffed up after deer season would think I was making it up, so that day stayed a secret between me and Uncle Akaa.

Then one day, after Uncle Akaa knew I would keep my finger outside the trigger guard until I was ready to shoot something, and keep the muzzle of my weapon pointed in a safe direction all the time, and focus on the front sight, and always check behind my intended target, and so on and so on, he produced my "graduation present."

"My domestic sister is very concerned that you learn to conduct yourself in polite society," he said. "Well, the great twentieth-century philosopher Robert Heinlein observed that 'an armed society is a polite society,' and I think you're ready for your debut.

"Your mom may have forgotten to mention it, but our mother, your Grams, and a girlfriend drove all the way across the country in 1947, from Oregon to Virginia, in a Packard touring car. To hear her tell it, she never had to take her .38 Special revolver out of the glove box."

Reaching into the small of his back, Uncle Akaa produced and handed me a semiautomatic pistol then watched approvingly as I made sure it was pointing downrange, found the lever to drop the magazine out of the grip, and slid back the slide, twice, to see that it was unloaded. It had sort of crappy brown plastic grips with a star and circle, and I recognized it from the foreign weapons class: a Russian Makarov, small and heavy and mean. Everything my Purdey over & under was not.

"This has brought me luck," said Uncle Akaa. "Luckiest of all when, like Grams, I had it but didn't need to take it out. So for now I'll keep it for you, until you're on your own and have a legal place to keep it. Meanwhile, I'll sleep better when your parents turn you loose on the crowded public roads with a high-speed projectile, tons of steel and gallons of explosives, knowing that you've already proved yourself responsible with other deadly instruments."

Well, after the guns you can just imagine how worked up Mom got last Christmas, when Uncle Akaa called to say he was coming to visit. He said he wanted to see me before I started visiting colleges in the spring. And how relieved she was when all he brought for me was books. Seven matching leather-bound volumes, from a printer in Lahore of all places, with fancy gilt titles down their spines: *Baghdad Sketches, Perseus in the Wind, Traveller's Prelude, Beyond Euphrates, The Coast of Incense, Dust in the Lion's Paw, and The Valleys of the Assassins.* All by an old Brit about traveling around the Middle East a century ago. Now *that* was exactly the kind of thing a young lady needs when heading off to college. And wouldn't those look fine over my desk in the dorm, when my roommates' parents came to visit?

Mom never actually opened any of the books, of course. She never discovered Freya Stark's wonderful ability, not to defy convention and authority but to dismiss them as irrelevant. The severe codes of the Arab and Persian worlds she explored, as well as the equally rigid mandates of British society in her time. She somehow lived outside both, and she addressed the most outrageous adventures with humor and irony:

> *"My education has been neglected in matters like arithmetic and correct behavior of many kinds, but I was properly brought up to worship fire."*

"...I spent a fortnight in that part of the country where one is less frequently murdered..."

"Did Shah Riza think I could be induced to smuggle across some opium when I returned to Iraq? I could not do that, said I decidedly.... I hoped to have plenty of crimes of my own to organize by that time."

And Mom never noticed my feral uncle's handwritten note inside the cover of *"Baghdad Sketches"*:

Dearest Gingat,

Enjoy, but responsibly. As our old friend Mr. Kipling said, "Words are, of course, the most powerful drug used by mankind."

Love,

Uncle Akaa

SULTAN OF SWAT

The matter began across the border. It shall finish
where God pleases. Here, in my own country, or
in hell. All three are one.

—Rudyard Kipling, *In Black and White*

SWAT VALLEY, PAKISTAN, 2009

U tilizing both lanes and seldom touching the brake, Brigadier
Sultan slalomed his Land Cruiser around potholes and
fallen boulders, while from the shotgun seat Colonel Bailey
looked almost straight down three hundred feet to the cascading
Swat River below. Bailey remembered this very spot, from twenty
years before: a gigantic, frog-shaped limestone boulder that split
the swift green torrent of the beautiful, dangerous mountain river
known in ancient Buddhist times as Suvastu, the White Serpent.

Colonel Bailey's old friend still relegated his driver to the back-
seat and drove himself, with the same élan as when he and Bailey

first had ranged up and down the Afghan border, then as majors. Gray streaks in Sultan's black hair and mustache, and a few extra pounds around his midriff, only added to the martial image of the cunning, barrel-chested Pakistani Special Services Group officer. He always had been a serious and passionate officer, but now Bailey sensed a new focus, something more than his promotion up the ranks to the responsibilities of a brigadier.

Pointing down the valley ahead, Sultan broke his long silence. "Five days ago, in lower Swat, an old schoolteacher was murdered by some of these thugs from Waziristan. They left a note on his body, forbidding anyone from moving or burying him for three days. The schoolteacher's son of course defied the threat and buried his father immediately, as required of all good Muslims. The Waziris returned that night, shot the son in front of his family, then dug up the old man's body and hung it from a power pole in the marketplace. When I drove by two days later, both bodies were still there, untouched. There were no more sons in the family.

"I ringed the town with soldiers, cut down the body, and gave both a proper Islamic burial. Later that evening," Sultan continued with a wolfish grin, "I posted snipers high on the hillside overlooking the graves, with powerful American night-vision scopes, to reinforce the will of Allah. Yesterday we sent two bodies back to the tribal elders in Waziristan for burial.

"These times are different. It is not just that this is now happening less than a hundred miles from the capital of my own country of Pakistan, from my home and family. There is a new brutality that goes against all the laws of Allah and of civilization." Brigadier

Sultan paused to navigate the SUV gingerly across a landslide, where the surging river had undercut its bank beneath the road and greedily consumed fifty feet of roadbed.

"I am not a professor or a commentator, but my idea is this," he continued. "The Pushtun tribals always have been very hard people, vicious fighters, and cruel to their enemies. But their feuds were over tribal things, and according to tribal customs. *Zan, zar, zamin*: women, gold, land. Honor, respect and revenge, and everything intensely personal. The most vicious feuds of all were those between cousins. Women and children, *mullahs* and schoolteachers were not the targets.

"But then came the terrible decade of the Russians, the Red Army. And they were brutal too, and cruel, but in a modern, bureaucratic, communist way. On orders from nameless men in Moscow, whole villages disappeared, from bombs and gas and mines. The Pushtuns lost their land, their women and children were dispersed to squalid camps in foreign countries, and the tribes lived, even made war, on the charity of strangers. So a generation of Mujahedin learned from, and grew more like, their new enemies. I hope the world never sees what the young Russian soldiers learned from the Pushtuns and took home to their own country."

The Land Cruiser continued its progress down the torturous valley, Bailey's attention drawn to the torrent that rushed almost beneath their tires; an incessant basso profundo rumble just at or below the audible; glimpses of deep-green swirling pools and gleaming ivory cascades. Just as the sun was disappearing over the mountains to their right and shadow began to engulf the river, they arrived at their destination for the night. The road turned left and crossed the river over a wood-decked steel bridge, its square prefab panels pinned together like a gigantic LEGO toy, developed by the British Army during World War II and now ubiquitous throughout the former empire, familiar to both Bailey and Sultan from combat engineer training as lieutenants. At its eastern end, a low white building hugged the bank between road and river, from which a deck cantilevered out over the gulf to overhang the swirling flow.

The small hotel and its wooden balcony, in its five-star scenic location, was also just as Bailey remembered, except it no longer catered to the occasional tourists and mountain climbers who got this far up the valley. Only the military could now enjoy its view and its respite from the spine-pounding road, and that only because a platoon of Frontier Corps Scouts had garrisoned there to secure the bridge. Bailey and Sultan leaned back in sturdy wooden chairs and watched a boy scramble down the riverbank, net in hand, to catch their dinner. Bailey knew that sizzling fat trout, split and fried, would arrive sooner or later, with pommes frites and probably a sparse salad of sliced tomato, cucumber, and onion. The proprietor would promise dinner at whatever time was requested, but it would arrive, in fact, according to its own schedule, not the diners'. Even Brigadier Sultan knew better than to try to influence events.

Bailey unscrewed the wide blue top from a Nalgene plastic water bottle and poured himself a generous shot of tea-colored Johnny Walker Red from the American Embassy commissary in Islamabad. Sultan never indulged, but neither did he mind when his non-Muslim friend did so. The old joke between them, for more than two decades now, was that although Bailey might be allowed an occasional sundowner, Sultan was compensated by being allowed four wives. When Sultan bemoaned the fact that he couldn't afford four wives anyway, Bailey commiserated that neither could he afford aged, single-malt Scotch.

The pair was soon joined by a third officer, a lean, mustachioed lieutenant colonel, his gray, long-tailed *shalwar* shirt gathered at the waist by a wide leather pistol belt. The silver badge of an ibex head on the side of his jaunty white, rolled wool cap identified him as a member of the renowned Gilgit Scouts from the Frontier Corps. He hugged Brigadier Sultan and greeted him as an old friend, then raised his eyebrows in surprise when he realized Colonel Bailey was American. "We seldom see our American friends so far from Islamabad," he said warmly. "Welcome to the most beautiful part of all Pakistan." His smile vanished. "Now we must rescue it."

Without further pleasantries, the Scouts officer unfolded a large, military topographic map and laid it across the tabletop, smiling again as he replaced Colonel Bailey's glass tumbler of "tea" at exactly the spot on the map that showed their location at the river crossing. Although he knew the region well, Bailey marveled at the maze of contour lines, each line depicting three hundred feet of elevation and so close together they almost merged into a solid brown color, and at the numerous blobs and ropes of white depicting glaciers and ice-covered mountaintops. Only on the southern edge of the map could be seen green expanses and the symbols for towns and villages. From here to the north and east stretched the region of Kohistan, the Land of Mountains, engulfing the Indus River Gorges, the Karakoram Range, and Nanga Parbat, The Naked Mountain, the western anchor of the Himalaya—as unforgiving as any place on Earth.

With the horn tip of his swagger stick, the Scouts officer traced a route down the road and river from their location, then up a side valley that led to the east. At a point ten kilometers up, he said, lay a shelter used by shepherds in the summer months, and it was there that two boys herding goats had seen Sultan's quarry.

"The boys are Gujars," he said. For Bailey's benefit, he explained, "These are a poor, semi-nomadic ethnic group. Mostly they herd goats and sheep in the mountains, and in the winter they live in their own villages, separate from other tribes. They know everything that is happening in the mountains, and they keep it to themselves. Their story only came to us through one of my scouts, who is also Gujar.

"I believe it must be good intelligence; they could not possibly make it up. The boys say they saw a strange small wizard, with a sparse gray beard and electric machines in the shelter, whose servant was an eight-foot-tall, black devil. There were also at least five ordinary, armed men. These Gujar children never have seen, or even heard of, black Africans, of course, but they know well the local legends of the *yush*. These are very tall, hairy devils, black or reddish in color, who live in the high mountains, like the yeti legends in Nepal. Here they say that in the old, pagan times the *yush* traded with men, and even had their own, primitive villages, but since the coming of Islam the *yush* shun all mankind. So the boys believe there is some great evil hatching in this valley, and their *mullah* brought them to his kinsman in my ranks."

"Out of the mouth of babes," murmured Bailey appreciatively.

The Scouts officer continued his briefing. "The trail from the Swat River up to the shepherds' hut can be driven partway by Jeep now, in the late summer, and that will be our route tomorrow morning, with a platoon of my Gilgit Scouts. Those in the hut will know the moment we leave the main valley road, of course, and probably flee. Up the mountain, there are only three foot-trails that lead out of the valley." Tapping the map again with his swagger stick, he ticked off each pass in turn: farthest east, directly over the mountains of Kohistan and down to the gorge of the Indus River; in the middle, south and east to the province of Bunar, on the west bank of the Indus; and last, south to the heart of Swat above the embattled city of Mingora. On the approach to each, the Gilgit Scouts had quietly inserted foot patrols; in the morning ambushes would cut off all flight.

Leaning forward intently, Brigadier Sultan spun the map so he saw the terrain as would the inhabitants of the shepherds' hut, facing the three trails. After long, silent moments staring at the convoluted lines, he reached out his left hand and stabbed a meaty forefinger directly onto the center pass. "There is where we will catch them, breaking for Bunar," he asserted with a tight smile.

"I hope you're right," replied the Scout commander. "The Scouts on that pass are all Ismailis from lower Gilgit. No wahabbis, human or devil, will talk, buy, or fight their way into Bunar tomorrow."

His briefing over, he leaned back in his seat, signaled his orderly to bring tea, and looked speculatively from Sultan to Bailey and back. "And now," he said with a grin, "perhaps you could fill me in about how this humble field soldier comes to be hosting exalted visitors from Army Headquarters in Rawalpindi. And elsewhere," he added with a glance at Colonel Bailey. "Why, within less than a day of my routine intelligence report, a helicopter delivers my old friend, unannounced, and his even less announced companion? We are living in strange, unsettled times. Could it be we actually have caught the elusive *yush*, a genuine devil? And even at Army Headquarters, where they know everything, how do they know which trail the devil will choose tomorrow?"

Brigadier Sultan picked up the thread. "Your *yush* is in fact a Somali—very tall, very dark, very deadly, but human. His companion, the wizard with the electronics, however, may be a devil, or at least a tool of *Shaitan*. He is an Egyptian Arab sometimes called Imam Rashid, a so-called religious instructor from al-Qa'ida. It was he who broadcast special guidance over a secret, shortwave radio to the young Taliban fanatics in Mingora, telling them to kill the schoolteacher a few days ago and to desecrate his body. He told those boys that it was their duty, that the old man was not a Muslim because he allowed girls to be taught in his school. May Imam Rashid burn in Hell forever—starting tomorrow—for sitting up here on his mountain, pretending to speak in the name of the Prophet—Peace Be Upon Him—directing ignorant boys to murder for Him, to die for Him."

Sultan took a deep breath to regain his temper, nodded toward Colonel Bailey, and continued in the flat monotone of a military briefing. "Colonel Bailey and I met these two years ago in Afghanistan during the jihad against the Soviets. We were both majors. They were murderous zealots even then, wanted to shoot us both, and we them, but that was not the right place, or season. I never believed it was over between us, and when I listened to our intercept of that shortwave order, I recognized the voice immediately— even though I had not heard it for twenty years. Then your report of wizards and devils arrived, and everything fell into place; I had what they call at the staff college in Quetta 'actionable intelligence,' a known identity at a known location in real time.

"These two are considered just rank-and-file al-Qa'ida, not what our American friends call HVTs, high-value targets, for whom they offer millions. But these two have threatened me, my friend and ally while he was my guest, and now my country. Worse, they have perverted the True Religion, and their ideas are a bigger threat than all the bomb makers in Pakistan, Afghanistan, and Iraq combined. My honor as a Pushtun, no less than my duty as an officer, demands but one response."

Again nodding to indicate Bailey, he continued, "I thought my old friend too might need a change from fighting this war from Washington and Islamabad and Kabul, where few now have ever heard a shot fired or seen an enemy die except on a flat-screen TV like a video game. Because he is the only other witness who could identify our Saudi and Somali cousins, I persuaded my headquarters to request that he join me for few days to conduct some 'basic research on the historical origins of al-Qa'ida.' The mountain air is good for two old soldiers."

At barely walking speed, the Scouts commander's Hilux truck crawled in four-wheel drive up the almost dry creek bed, followed fifty meters back by Brigadier Sultan and Colonel Bailey in their Land Cruiser, more trucks with Scouts perched in the beds spaced out ahead and behind. Well before dawn they had assembled in the hotel courtyard, silently but for the occasional clank of a weapon hitting a vehicle side and the murmur of the NCOs making their rounds, checking their men and equipment. Bailey sensed Sultan's suppressed excitement and savored the copper taste of adrenaline in his own mouth.

With only parking lights showing, they had rolled down the still, dark valley, and even the river, looming invisible on their right, seemed quieter in the predawn hush, more a hiss than its daytime rumble. Halting where the track that led to the shepherds' hut cut left from the Swat Valley road, they dismounted most of the force and watched as the silent files disappeared up the goat tracks. When the first gray dawn allowed the vehicles to pick their way forward without headlights, the Scouts commander and his small headquarters element, together with Brigadier Sultan and Colonel Bailey, followed.

Inside the lurching vehicle, Bailey turned to Sultan. "I'm curious to know why you were so certain last night that our targets will try to escape to Bunar. You skipped that part of the explanation."

Sultan flashed his friend a grin. "Sometimes a little mystery, and a reputation for foresight, can be useful in a commanding officer. But really, I'm quite confident based on history. Most of my colleagues, and yours, think this conflict with militant Wahabbist

Islam began on September 11, 2001, or perhaps when American forces went into Saudi Arabia during the Gulf War, or perhaps when the Arabs came to Afghanistan to join the Jihad in the 1980s. In fact this is but a battle in a war that dates back centuries."

"In the nineteenth century, Swat, Bunar, and Kohistan fell just beyond the borders of the British Empire, which ended at the Indus River. It was on the eastern slopes of the great massif of Mahabun Mountain in Bunar that powerful clandestine networks of militant Islamists from across the Empire, with their epicenter at Patna on the Ganges River, working directly with Wahabbis in Saudi Arabia, established the fortress of Sittana. There they trained and equipped young zealots for armed insurrections, suicide missions, and assassinations, exactly as al-Qa'ida did in Taliban-ruled Afghanistan. Then, as in our own time, this had powerful religious as well as military significance.

"Do you remember Imam Rashid snarling at us in Afghanistan so many years ago? Even though we supposedly were fighting for the same goal, he called us infidels, said it was sacred ground, a place of jihad, where they would die as martyrs and where we had no right to be. These wahabbis believe that a true and successful jihad can only be launched from a pure Islamic state, ruled by a holy and absolute caliph. The deeds of their jihad are conducted secretly, and in the enemy camp, of course, by all means fair and foul, but they believe that having that sacred base justifies their evil actions. That is the importance of Mullah Omar and Afghanistan to al-Qa'ida, and so it was with Mahabun Mountain two centuries ago.

"And today as well. Many of those from al-Qa'ida who escaped the bombing at Tora Bora in Afghanistan in 2001 made their way to Sittana, where they lay low in the old 'holy' sanctuary until their trail turned cold. Our two cousins here were in that number, and that is why I believe they will seek refuge there again when pursued." Sultan glanced directly at his old ally. "I only learned all this last year. If others knew as it was happening, they chose not to share the information."

The rest of Sultan's thoughts remained unspoken, as a bright flash of light twenty meters to their right was followed instantly by a violent rocking of the Toyota and the loud crump of an exploding shell, whether mortar or rocket-propelled grenade Bailey could not tell. Even before the hail of rock and shrapnel finished rattling on the vehicle's roof and hood, Bailey and Sultan flung open the doors and, weapons in hand, trotted hastily to the side, away from the boulder-strewn creek bed that was clearly the gunner's target.

As Bailey focused intently to keep his footing on the round, water-polished stones of the creek bed, another part of him was acutely aware of the pungent smell of high explosive, the ozone smell of fractured rock, and the tangy sagebrush smell of vegetation underfoot. A second explosive round pounded into the ground an equal distance left of the Scouts commander's vehicle ahead, and with a familiar chill Bailey knew that the next, if the gunner were good, would be centered directly between the two.

Instead, from out of sight ahead, a single, slow burst of automatic rifle fire rang out, then swelled to a crescendo as weapon after weapon joined in and echoes reverberated off the valley walls. Stray rounds buzzed overhead, then quickly tapered off as the fires of the Scouts foot patrols gained the upper hand. Bailey recalled Sultan pointing out to him on a previous occasion that the Pushtu word for the sound of a gunshot, *"daz,"* expressed the sound from the point of view of the target, while the English "bang" was closer to that of the shooter.

Standing outside the low stone walls of the shepherds' shelter, Sultan and Bailey slowly took in the three bodies, laid out on their backs in a row, and the three prisoners who squatted silently under the muzzles of watchful Scouts. All six wore military camouflage jackets and trousers, unkempt black beards, and long hair that fell over their ears and collars. From the partially collapsed roof of the hut, a wire antenna extended thirty feet horizontally in both directions, terminating in wooden poles that held it in the air. Its bare wire dangled through the roof, no longer attached to anything inside. The Scouts already had removed a quantity of weapons and ammunition, and all that remained were a large soot-blackened cooking pot and a half-full, hundred-pound bag of rice.

The Scouts commander joined the pair. "Thank God. We took no casualties," he announced. "But no devils either. And our assumption that these guys would flee was a bit hasty, wasn't it?"

"Perhaps," agreed Colonel Bailey. "At Tora Bora, too, dozens stayed behind and died in the caves to cover the escape of the al-Qa'ida elite."

From far up the valley, to their south and east, a volley of rifle fire echoed and reechoed as it rolled down the valley toward them.

It trailed off, to be followed by two, more muted, pops spaced about a minute apart.

Some time later and twelve hundred vertical feet higher, muscles burned in Bailey's calves and thighs from the adrenalin-fueled rush up the valley to the pass. He hoped Sultan and the Scouts had not noticed the slight "sewing-machine" tremble that possessed his left ankle. When he was certain his breathing had returned to normal, Bailey broke the silence. "Ever since our incident on the border, I've watched for these two in every valley, every bazaar, every intelligence report. Of course, I had no names, no photographs, just a memory. Over time I'd lost faith that I'd ever track them down. I thought perhaps they were already dead.

"And, for a decade I've observed the dangerous emergence of Imam Rashid. I've read his *fatwas*, seen their bloody results, and lost a brave friend at his murderous direction. But for him, too, we had no true name, no photograph or description. Always it was text translations I was studying, never original recordings, so I never made the voice connection as you did. Thank you, brother. *To every thing there is a season, and a time to every purpose under the heaven.*"

"My people say it a little differently," replied Sultan. "*If a Pushtun gets his revenge after one hundred years, he still regrets his haste.*"

In front of Brigadier Sultan's Land Cruiser, hillsides gradually pulled back from the road and turned a lusher green. To their right the river slowed and broadened its bed, tracing a network of narrow braided channels around shifting islands of gravel and sand.

Two men worked their way across on a crude wooden raft, avoiding the islands of damp, water-darkened sand—quicksand traps created by the grinding glaciers of the Himalaya, polished and deposited by the summer floods of the White Serpent. Ahead the road led through the fertile poppy fields of lower Swat, over the Malakand Pass into the Vale of Peshawar, and on to the wide, tree-lined avenues of Islamabad.